J. Brander Matthews

Comedies for Amateur Acting

J. Brander Matthews

Comedies for Amateur Acting

ISBN/EAN: 9783744784740

Printed in Europe, USA, Canada, Australia, Japan

Cover: Foto ©Andreas Hilbeck / pixelio.de

More available books at **www.hansebooks.com**

APPLETONS' NEW HANDY-VOLUME SERIES.

COMEDIES

FOR

AMATEUR ACTING,

EDITED, WITH A PREFATORY NOTE ON PRIVATE THEATRICALS,

BY

J. BRANDER MATTHEWS.

NEW YORK:

D. APPLETON AND COMPANY,

1880.

À

M. PAUL FERRIER,

TÉMOIGNAGE DE CONFRATERNITÉ.

J. B. M.

CONTENTS.

PREFATORY NOTE.

AN aspiring amateur actor once asked a celebrated dramatic critic, "What did you think of the performance of our club?" And the cruel critic is said to have answered, slowly and with a slight drawl, "I should hardly have called it a club; it seemed to me more like a collection of sticks."

At another private performance, it was either Garrick or Kean who exclaimed involuntarily, "There is an actor," when the footman of the play presented a letter and it turned out that, none of the amateurs being willing to accept so small a part, a professional "utility man" had been engaged from the theatre. The player was probably not the equal of his noble and gentle associates in intelligence or in education, but he knew his business. And it was his business—for them it was only amusement. Yet many of them were doubtless told, and some of them perhaps believed, that they had only to desire success on the stage to find it within their grasp. They believed, in short, that they could be actors if they chose; in truth, they were only amateurs. Charles Lamb reports Coleridge as having said: "There is an infinity of trick in all that Shakspere wrote: I could write like Shakspere if I had a mind." And Lamb adds quietly: "So, you see, Coleridge only lacked the mind." The application to amateur actors is obvious.

Macready remarks that, with one exception, the only amateur he had seen "with any pretensions to theatrical talent was Charles Dickens, of world-wide fame." Now it was not jealousy, as some vain amateurs would fain believe, which led Macready to write thus. He was not above the feeling, as his journal plainly shows, nor was Garrick or Kean. But he and they, like all actors who have won fame and fortune by hard work, had a feeling akin to contempt for those who dabbled for mere amusement in the art of acting, to which they had given a lifetime of study. They knew that without long labor nothing is likely to be achieved in the art which is, to a certain extent at least, the union of all other arts. Campbell condensed pages of prose discussion into a few beautiful lines:

> "For ill can Poetry express
>   Full many a tone of thought sublime;
> And Painting, mute and motionless,
>   Steals but a glance of time.
> But by the mighty actor brought,
>   Illusion's perfect triumphs come;
> Verse ceases to be airy thought,
>   And Sculpture to be dumb."

"It surely," Macready comments, "needs something like an education for such an art, and yet that appearance of mere volition and perfect ease, which costs the accomplished artist so much time and toil to acquire, evidently leads to a different conclusion with many, or amateur acting would be less in vogue." Although the theatre is a place of amusement for the lawyer and the doctor, it is the workshop of the actor, and his work there is just as hard for him as the doctor's or the lawyer's is in his study.

Few would presume to paint elaborate historical pictures without years of training—without the study of perspective, of anatomy, of the handling of colors, of the thousand and one other things which the task demands. .Yet we find not a few, with as little preparation as possible, bravely battling with Hamlet and Richelieu, and retiring amid the plaudits of their friends, convinced that they only need a wider field to rival Booth or the memory of Kean and Kemble. There is unfortunately nothing in the art of acting as simple as the sketch of which the amateur in the art of design can acquit himself without discredit. A sketch, as its name suggests, may be the happy record of a fleeting impression, slight and incomplete; but a play, even the lightest little comedy, be it never so short, is a complete and finished whole, containing at least one situation plainly presented and pushed to its logical conclusion. The demand it makes on the actor is as great in quality, although not in quantity, as the demand made by five acts.

But the desire for the drama, and for taking part in it, is apparently innate in most of us. Possibly a passion for mimicry is the survival of a tendency to monkey tricks inherited from some simian ancestor who hung, suspended by his prehensile tail, from the boughs of the forest primeval. Or, as the English poet, Mr. Edmund W. Gosse, has neatly put it: "The taste for acting seems inherent in the human mind. Perhaps there is no imaginative nature that does not wish, at one time or another, to step into the person of another, to precipitate his own intelligence on the action of a different mind, to contemplate from the interior, instead of always observing the exterior. To act a part is to widen the sympathy, to increase the experience, and hence the diversion of private theatricals has been held to be no small part of education by some of the most serious of men." Amateur acting has, in fact, its advantages, needless to be specified here. It is well, therefore, to study how to make the best use of these advantages, and to turn private theatricals to profit, as best we may. First of all, the amateur should never choose a play which has been recently acted by professional actors. The amateur, however good, can hardly hope to equal the professional, however poor. So he must needs avoid the comparison. Discretion is the better part of valor, and private theatricals are in themselves a feat foolhardy enough to be the better for an extra portion of discretion. They call for all the help they can get, so they should never neglect the advantage of novelty in the chosen play. The interest the spectators feel in the unfolding of the plot may thus be reflected upon the actors.

In the second place, it is the duty of the amateur to choose as short a play as possible. A piece in one act is far less likely to fatigue the spectators than a piece in five acts. And the shortness is a great boon to the amateur, who lacks many things needed in a long play—the knowledge, for instance, of how to use his voice without fatigue. There is no limit to the variety of subject and style to be found within the compass of one act. You can have comedy, farce, burlesque, extravaganza, drama, opera, and even tragedy—and all in one brief act. One of the most effective situations in the modern drama of France— a situation so striking that it has been stolen half a dozen times—is to be found in a play in one act, " La Joie fait Peur," of Mme. de Girardin. Indeed, the French excel in the writing of one-act plays, even as they excel just now in the writing of plays of almost every kind. Many of their lighter comedies in one act are admirably adapted for amateur acting; the characters are well marked, the dialogue is flowing and in general not exacting, and the scenery and mounting can easily be compassed by a little ingenuity and perseverance. Indeed, the scene is in most cases laid in a parlor, with the costumes of every-day life. Now in such costumes, and in such scenes, and in short plays like these, the amateur is seen at his best. When he is ambitious, and tries to do "Hamlet" or "The Lady of Lyons," or even "The Hunchback" or "The Honeymoon," he is seen at his worst. And when the amateur is bad, it is often because he is bumptious. All amateurs are not bumptious, and all amateurs therefore are not bad. And amateurs who are not bad because they are not bumptious, wisely and modestly gauge their own strength, and refuse incontinently to do battle with any ponderous monster in five acts.

It has been held by some wise critics that the best programme for an amateur performance is a two-act comedy, followed by a one-act farce or comedietta, or even burlesque; the more serious play of course coming first, and the lighter later—like the sweet after the roast. Where the evening's entertainment consists of Mrs. Jarley's waxworks or tableaux, together with a play, the play should always be given first, in order that the spectators shall see it before they are wearied and worn by the multitudinous delays which always accompany a series of tableaux, however excellently ordered or frequently rehearsed. Although the experiment is a rash one, a three-act play may sometimes be substituted by experienced amateurs for the two plays, with a total of

three acts. There are many good three-act plays, light
and bright, and well suited for parlor performance. The
influence of Mr. Robertson, the author of "Caste," and
of his host of imitators in the teacup-and-saucer school
of comedy, has given us a long list of three-act pieces just
about worthy of amateur acting. There are unfortunately but few good two-act plays—"Simpson & Co.,"
the "Sweethearts" of Mr. W. S. Gilbert, and half a
dozen more. And equally unfortunate is it that, while
one-act plays must be the staple of private theatricals,
nearly all the really good comedies of that length have
been acted so often that they are thoroughly hackneyed.
As there is no professional demand for pieces in one
act—managers for some reason or other seeming to be
afraid of them—the amateur demand does not call forth
an equal supply. It is for amateurs, however, that the
half-dozen one-act plays in this little book have been
prepared.

One of the comedies which follow, "A Bad Case," is
wholly original, having been kindly written for this volume by my friends Mr. Julian Magnus and Mr. H. C.
Bunner, working together, as was the custom in the days
of Beaumont and Fletcher. The other five little plays
are "not translations—only taken from the French," as
Sneer smartly phrases it in "The Critic." Some of them
follow the French originals with more or less closeness,
while others are indebted only for the suggestion or
skeleton of the plot. In a different shape, three of the
five plays have already appeared in "Appletons' Journal" and in "Puck," but all have been carefully revised
for this volume. The title of each of the French comedies thus adapted and the name of the author appear
at the head of each play. The authors laid under con-

tribution are M. Eugène Labiche, the leading comic dramatist of France; M. Mario Uchard, the author of many charming fantasies; M. Paul Ferrier, one of the foremost of the younger dramatic authors of France; the late Henry Mürger, the tender singer of a Bohemia which now is not; and M. de Bornier, the author of the "Fille de Roland," almost the only tragedy which has of late years been successful in France.

The piece of absurdity, "Heredity," is a simple bit of fooling of slight pretensions, and printed here to afford an opportunity to amateurs of gratifying the prevailing taste for light musical plays. The words of a few songs in common metres are given, for which fitting music can easily be found either in the lighter operas or among the airs of the day: they may be omitted, and other songs inserted at any point. The play is offered merely as a framework on which the actors may hang what they will—a vehicle for the exhibition of any special accomplishments, singing, dancing, or what not, in which the amateurs who attempt it may be proficient: no apology is therefore needed for its literary demerits.

These plays may all be acted free of charge by amateurs. Professional performers who may desire to produce any of them will please communicate with the editor through the publishers.

A TRUMPED SUIT.

COMEDY IN ONE ACT.

By JULIAN MAGNUS.

CHARACTERS.

M. CARBONEL.

VICTOR DELILLE.

ANATOLE GARADOUX.

CÉCILE, *Carbonel's daughter.*

ANNETTE, *chambermaid.*

[The French original of this play is " *Les Deux Timides,*" written by M. Eugène Labiche.]

A TRUMPED SUIT.

SCENE. Salon in a country house near Paris. Large doors at back supposed to open on a garden. Door L. I. E. Doors L. 2 E. and R. 2 E. Mantelpiece R. Clock and vases on mantel. Table with writing materials L. R., a small ornamental table. Small sideboard against wall L. Usual furniture of a handsome salon.

At rise of curtain, Annette, with hot-water jug in her hand, comes from back, opens door L. 2 E., and deposits the jug within.

ANNETTE.

Monsieur, there is the hot water. [*Comes front.*] This M. Anatole Garadoux, mademoiselle's intended, is what I call queer. He wouldn't suit me at all. Every morning, he takes an hour and a half to dress himself and polish his nails—that is, half an hour to dress, and an hour to trim his nails. He has a case of little instruments, and cuts, and scrapes, and grinds, and rubs, and files, *and* powders, *and* polishes—what a housemaid he'd have

2

been if Fate hadn't spoiled him at the start! . I
don't know what M. Carbonel can have seen in him!
Oh, my! I suppose master could no more say
"no" to him than he can to any one about anything. It's absurd that a man of his age should
have no more will than a baby. He hasn't any
more firmness than jelly in the sunshine! His
daughter makes up for him, though. With all her
sweetly innocent, yielding manner, she has her
own way when she wants it. [*Cécile is heard
singing in the garden.*] She's coming back from
her morning walk.

CÉCILE, *entering at back with a lot of cut flowers in her apron.*

Annette, bring the vases.

ANNETTE, *taking vases to table.*

Yes, mademoiselle. [*They busy themselves
arranging the flowers.*] He's getting up. I have
just taken in the hot water.

CÉCILE.

To whom?

ANNETTE.

To M. Garadoux.

CÉCILE.

What does that matter to me?

ANNETTE.

Have you noticed his nails?

CÉCILE, *curtly*.

No!

ANNETTE.

Not noticed his nails! Why they're as long as that. But the other day, in trying to open a window, he broke one.

CÉCILE, *ironically*.

Poor nail!

ANNETTE.

To be sure, it will grow again—in time; but wasn't he cross? Since then, he has always rung for me to open the window.

CÉCILE.

I have already had to ask you not to be for ever talking to me about M. Garadoux—it is disagreeable! it annoys me!

ANNETTE, *astonished*.

Your intended!

CÉCILE.

Intended, yes; but intentions don't always lead to—marriage. Where is papa?

[*Replaces vase on mantel.*

ANNETTE.

In his study; he's been there more than an hour with a gentleman who came from Paris—

CÉCILE, *quickly*.

From Paris ?   A young man — a lawyer ?
Blond—very quiet manner—blue eyes ?

ANNETTE.

No.   This one is dark, has mustaches—and a
beard like a blacking-brush.

CÉCILE, *disappointed*.

Ah !

ANNETTE.

I fancy he's a traveler for a wine-merchant.
Your father didn't want to see him, but he managed to squeeze through the door with his bottles.

CÉCILE.

Why doesn't papa send him away ?

ANNETTE.

M. Carbonel ?   He's too timid to do that.
[*Places other vase on mantel.*

CÉCILE.

I am afraid he is.

CARBONEL, *speaking outside R. 2 E.*

Monsieur, it is I who am indebted to you
—delighted ! [*Enters with two small bottles.*]   I didn't want it, but I have bought four
casks.

CÉCILE.

You have bought more wine ?

ANNETTE.

The cellar is full. [*Goes up.*

CARBONEL.

I know it; but how could I say "no" to a man who was so nicely dressed—who had just come twelve miles—on purpose to offer me his wine ? In fact, he put himself to great inconvenience to come here.

CÉCILE.

But it's you he has inconvenienced.

ANNETTE, *at back.*

The great point is, is the wine good.

CARBONEL.

Taste it.

ANNETTE, *after pouring some into glass which she takes from sideboard, drinks, and utters cry of disgust.*

CARBONEL.

That's exactly how it affected me. I even ventured to say to him—with extreme politeness —"Your wine seems to me a little young"; but I was afraid he was beginning to feel vexed—so I took four casks—only four !

ANNETTE, *taking the samples.*

Well, I'll use these for salads. [*Bell heard L.*]
That's M. Garadoux ringing for me to open his
window.   [*Exit L. 2 E.*

CARBONEL.

What! has M. Garadoux only just got up?

CÉCILE.

Yes, he never appears before ten o'clock.

CARBONEL.

That doesn't astonish me.   Every evening he
seizes my paper, as soon as it is left, and takes it
to his own room.   I believe he reads himself to
sleep.

CÉCILE.

And you don't see it?

CARBONEL.

Oh, yes, I do—the next day.

CÉCILE.

This is too bad.

CARBONEL.

I own I miss it; and if you could manage to
give him a hint—without its seeming to come from
me—

CÉCILE.

I'll give him a hint he can't misunderstand.

CARBONEL.

What ! you're not afraid ?

CÉCILE, *firmly*.

Afraid—of a man who wants to be my husband ?
Should I have agreed to think about him, if I was ?

CARBONEL.

I admire your spirit—and you only eighteen.
You're braver than I. The visit of this stranger
worries and bothers me.

CÉCILE.

Poor papa !

CARBONEL.

Thank Heaven, it will soon be over !

CÉCILE.

What ?

CARBONEL.

Why, all these visitors with their eternal offers.
They make me ill. What can you expect ? I
have passed my life in the Archive Office—in the
Secret Department. No one was ever admitted
there. That exactly suited me. Now I can't bear
to talk to people I don't know.

CÉCILE.

Then you know M. Garadoux well ?

CARBONEL.

Not at all ; my lawyer recommends him high-

ly, though, to be sure, he's only lately been my
lawyer.   M. Garadoux presented himself boldly—
we talked for two hours—that is, I with difficulty
managed to get in four words. He put questions,
and answered himself—and, you see, I felt quite
at my ease with him.

CÉCILE.

What were the four words you did get in ?

CARBONEL.

I promised him your hand—at least, he says
so.   Thereupon, he installed himself here—that
was a fortnight ago ; and to-day we have to go to
the mayor's office to publish the bans.

CÉCILE.

To-day ?

CARBONEL.

He fixed to-day—he settles everything.

CÉCILE.

But, papa—

CARBONEL.

Well ?

CÉCILE.

Do you like this M. Garadoux ?

CARBONEL.

He seems a very nice young man—and he can
talk by the hour together.

CÉCILE.

He's a widower; and I don't want a second-hand husband.

CARBONEL.

But—

CÉCILE.

Never mind your *but*. Listen to my *but*, which is, Suppose another suitor should appear?

CARBONEL.

What! Another!! More talking; more inquiries—begin all over again? No! No!! No!!!

[*Sits L. of table.*

CÉCILE.

The one I mean is not a stranger—you know him well—M. Victor Delille, a lawyer—

CARBONEL.

A lawyer! I never could bear to talk to a lawyer.

CÉCILE.

He is godmamma's nephew.

CARBONEL, *testily*.

I don't know him. I have never seen him.

CÉCILE.

Oh, papa! I thought godmamma had written to you—

CARBONEL.

That was three months ago—before Garadoux came. It was only a faint suggestion ; and since this Garadoux presented himself, I don't believe the other has ever thought of you.

CÉCILE.

Oh, yes, papa. I am sure he has.

CARBONEL.

Oh, indeed ! So you are sure, are you ? Come here. Tell me frankly what has he said to you.

CÉCILE, *sitting on his knee.*

Nothing, papa !—that is, nothing about love. But on the day of aunt's birthday dinner—when you wouldn't go, you know—

CARBONEL.

I don't like parties—that is, when there are people there.

CÉCILE.

I was sitting next M. Delille—and he kept blushing, and doing awkward things.

CARBONEL, *aside.*

I can feel for him. [*Aloud*] What did he do ?

CÉCILE.

He broke a wine-glass.

CARBONEL.

That's a stupidity—not a symptom.

CÉCILE.

Afterward, when I asked him for water, he passed me the salt-cellar.

CARBONEL.

Perhaps he is deaf.

CÉCILE.

Oh, no, papa, he is not deaf; he was nervous.

CARBONEL.

Well?

CÉCILE.

Well, when a young man—a lawyer—accustomed to speak in public—gets nervous because he is near a young lady, why [*lowering her eyes*] —there must be some cause.

CARBONEL.

And this cause must have been love for you?

CÉCILE, *rising.*

Oh, papa, suppose it was!

CARBONEL, *rising.*

If it had been, he would have come here. He has not come, so it was not love; perhaps it was dyspepsia ! I am very glad he didn't appear, for, as matters stand with M. Garadoux—

ANNETTE, *entering at back.*

The postman just left this letter, monsieur.

[*Exit.*

CÉCILE, *quickly.*

Godmamma's writing !

CARBONEL.

Don't get excited. Another invitation, I suppose. Why can't people leave me alone ? [*Reads*] "Dear M. Carbonel : Allow me to present to you M. Victor Delille, my nephew, about whom I spoke to you some months ago. He loves our dear Cécile—"

CÉCILE, *joyfully.*

I knew he did ! What did I tell you, papa ?

CARBONEL.

Here's a pretty dilemma ! [*Reads*] "His ardent desire is to obtain her hand. I had hoped to accompany him to-day, but illness prevents ; and he will therefore go to you alone."

CÉCILE.

He is coming here !

CARBONEL.

I shall go out at once.

CÉCILE, *reproachfully*.

Oh, papa !

CARBONEL.

What can I do ? I have given my word to M. Garadoux. You plunge me into unheard-of difficulties.

CÉCILE.

I'll extricate you, papa !

CARBONEL.

How ? What am I to do, badgered and bullied by two suitors ?

CÉCILE.

You sha'n't have two ; you must give M. Garadoux his dismissal.

CARBONEL.

I ! [*Seeing Garadoux entering from his room.*] Hush ! here he is !

GARADOUX.

Good morning, dear papa !

CARBONEL, *bowing*.

Monsieur Garadoux—

GARADOUX, *bowing to Cécile*.

My charming *fiancée*, you are as fresh this morning as a bunch of cherries.

CÉCILE.

A pretty compliment to my freshness—on *other* mornings.   [*She goes to table.*

CARBONEL, *aside.*

She's in too great a hurry. [*Aloud*] My dear M. Garadoux, have you slept well ?

GARADOUX.

Excellently. [*To Cécile*] I am up a little late, perhaps.

CÉCILE.

I did not reproach you.

CARBONEL.

The fact is, you don't like the country in the morning. [*Quickly*] I don't mean to find fault.

GARADOUX.

I ? Where is there such a magnificent picture as Nature's awakening ? The flowers expand their petals ; the blades of grass raise their heads to salute the rising sun. [*He looks at his nails.*] The butterfly dries his wings, still moist with the kisses of night. [*Draws a small instrument from his pocket and begins to file a nail.*]

CÉCILE, *aside.*

He's making this a dressing-room.

GARADOUX, *continuing to use file.*

The busy bee commences his visits to the rose, while the sweet-voiced linnet—

CÉCILE, *aside.*

Too much natural history ! [*Brusquely*] What news was there in the paper ?

GARADOUX.

What paper ?

CÉCILE.

Last night's—you took it—papa wasn't able to get a look at it.

CARBONEL, *aside.*

What nerve she has !

GARADOUX.

A thousand pardons, M. Carbonel. I took it inadvertently.

CARBONEL.

It is not the slightest consequence.

GARADOUX, *taking paper from his pocket, offers it to Carbonel.*

I haven't even unfolded it.

CARBONEL.

Oh, if you haven't read it, pray keep it, M. Garadoux.

GARADOUX, *offering it.*

No, I beg you will—

CARBONEL, *refusing it.*

I entreat you to keep it.

GARADOUX.

Since you insist! [*Puts it back in pocket, then goes to glass over mantel and adjusts his cravat.*]

CARBONEL, *aside.*

I should have liked, though, to see how stocks were going.

ANNETTE, *entering, hands card.*

This gentleman wants to see you.

CÉCILE, *coming quickly to Carbonel.*

A gentleman! [*Looking at card.*] 'Tis he!

CARBONEL, *low.*

The devil! And the other one here! What is to be done?

CÉCILE, *low.*

You can't send him away. [*Loud to Annette*] Ask him to walk up! [*Exit Annette.*

GARADOUX.

A visitor! Don't forget, father-in-law, that we have to be at the mayor's at noon.

CARBONEL.

Certainly! Of course! [*Low to Cécile*] Get *him* out of here.

CÉCILE.

Will you accompany me, M. Garadoux?

GARADOUX.

Delighted—where?

CÉCILE.

To water the flowers.

GARADOUX, *coldly.*

The sun is terribly hot.

CÉCILE.

The more reason not to keep the flowers waiting. Come!

GARADOUX.

Delighted!

CÉCILE, *aside.*

I'll make him break another nail!
[*Exeunt Cécile and Garadoux, at back.*

CARBONEL, *alone.*

Was there ever such a situation? One suitor accepted—staying here—and the other—a lawyer, too—how he will talk—he's sure to make me say what I don't mean. I know what I am—he'll

3

force me to say "Yes"—and then the other. Oh, if two affirmatives would only make a negative !

ANNETTE, *announcing at back.*
M. Delille.   [*Exit R.*

CARBONEL, *frightened.*

What shall I say to him ? [*Looks at his clothes.*]   Ah ! Can't receive him in a dressing-gown. I'll go and put on a coat.

[*Disappears L. I. E., as Delille enters at back.*

DELILLE, *coming forward very timidly, bows low.*

Monsieur — madame — I have the honor— [*Looks round.*] What, no one ! How glad I am ! I do hate to meet any one. I positively shudder at the idea of seeing this father, who knows I want to take away his daughter. [*Warmly*] How I love her ! Ever since that dinner when I broke a glass, I have been coming to this place every day to ask for her hand. I come by the mid-day train, but I can't summon up courage to ring the bell, and I go back by the next. Once I felt bold enough to ring, but then I ran away and hid round the corner. If this had been going to con-tinue, I should have bought a commutation ticket. To-day I am brave ; I have crossed the threshold —without my aunt, who was to have brought me, and now all alone I am going— [*Frightened*] Can

I do it ?   Is it possible to say to a man one doesn't know, "Give me your daughter to take to my house, and—" [*Shuddering.*]   No ! one can't do such things—at least, I can't.   [*Suddenly*] If I ran away !   No one has seen me !   I will—I can return to-morrow—by the same train.

[*About to exit back, meets Cécile entering.*

DELILLE, *stopping.*

Too late !

CÉCILE, *pretending surprise.*

I'm not mistaken !   M. Victor Delille.

DELILLE, *nervous.*

Yes, monsieur—that is, mademoiselle—

CÉCILE.

To what chance do we owe the honor of this call ?

DELILLE.

A mere chance—I was going by—I was looking for a notary—I saw a bell—and I rang it—it was a mistake.   [*Bowing.*]   Mademoiselle, I have the honor to say good-by.

CÉCILE.

Pray wait ; my father will be delighted to see you.

DELILLE.

Don't disturb him—some other time—

CÉCILE.

No, no! He would scold me. Won't you sit down?

DELILLE, *falling into chair.*

Thank you—I'm not tired. [*Pulls gloves on and off quickly.*]

CÉCILE, *aside.*

`Poor fellow! How nervous he is!

DELILLE, *aside.*

How pretty she is!

CÉCILE.

Will you excuse me if I fill my sugar-bowl? [*Goes to sideboard, where there is box of sugar and bowl.*]

DELILLE, *rising.*

If I am in your way, allow me to—

CÉCILE.

Not at all—if I might venture, I would ask you—

DELILLE.

What, mademoiselle?

CÉCILE.

To hold the bowl for me.

DELILLE.

Enchanted ! [*He takes bowl.*]　[*Aside*] If the father found us like this ! I must say something to her. I mustn't seem like an idiot. [*Aloud*] Mademoiselle Cecile !

CÉCILE, *encouragingly.*

Monsieur Victor ?

DELILLE, *hesitatingly.*

Your sugar is very white !

CÉCILE.

Like all sugars—

DELILLE, *tenderly.*

Oh, no ! Not like other sugars.

CÉCILE, *aside.*

Why does he want to talk about sugar ?

DELILLE, *aside.*

I have been too bold ! [*Aloud*] Is it cane or beet-root ?

CÉCILE.

I don't know the difference.

DELILLE.

There's a great deal ! One is—much more so than the other—

CÉCILE, *looking at him with wonder.*

Ah! thank you.   [*Takes bowl from him and goes to sideboard.*]

DELILLE, *aside.*

Why the deuce did I go out of my depth in sugars?

CÉCILE, *seeing Carbonel entering L.*

Here is papa!

DELILLE.

Oh, Heavens!

CÉCILE.

Papa, this is M. Victor Delille.   [*The two men are at opposite corners of the stage, and do not dare to look at one another.*]

CARBONEL, *aside.*

Here goes!   [*Bowing.*]   Monsieur — I am very glad — certainly —

DELILLE.

It is I — monsieur — who — am — certainly —

CARBONEL, *stealing a glance at him, aside.*

He looks very determined!

DELILLE, *aside.*

I wish I had got away!

CÉCILE.

You gentlemen have doubtless something to say to one another. I will leave you.

CARBONEL AND DELILLE.

No, no !

CÉCILE.

I must attend to my household duties. [*To Delille*] Sit down ! [*To Carbonel*] Sit down ! [*They both sit opposite each other.*] [*Low to Delille*] Be brave ! [*Low to Carbonel*] Be brave !

[*Exit L. I. E.*

CARBONEL, *aside.*

Here we are alone, and he seems quite at his ease.

DELILLE, *aside.*

I never was so nervous. [*Aloud*] Monsieur—

CARBONEL.

Monsieur— [*Aside*] I know he's going to ask for her.

DELILLE.

You have no doubt received a letter from my aunt.

CARBONEL.

A charming lady ! How is she ?

DELILLE.

Very well, indeed—that is—except her rheumatism, which has kept her in bed for a week.

CARBONEL.

That's all right—I mean I hope it will be, soon.

DELILLE.

I trust so, with warmer weather—

CARBONEL, *quickly*.

My barometer is going up.

DELILLE.

And mine, too—how strange that our barometers should agree so well!

CARBONEL.

It will burn up my roses, though.

DELILLE.

You are fond of roses?

CARBONEL.

Passionately. I cultivate them quite extensively.

DELILLE.

So do I.

CARBONEL.

That's all right. [*Aside*] So far we get on well.

DELILLE, *aside*.

He seems jovial! Suppose I— [*Aloud, ris-*

ing, very nervous] In her letter—my aunt—informed you that I was coming—

CARBONEL, *aside, rising.*

He's going to do it ! [*Aloud*] Well—you see —yes—but she did not clearly indicate the reason that—

DELILLE.

What ! she did not write that I—

CARBONEL.

No, not a word about that.

DELILLE, *aside.*

The devil ! Why, then—oh, this makes it ten times worse ! [*Aloud, with great effort*] Monsieur—I tremble while I ask—

CARBONEL, *trying to turn the conversation.*

What a sun ! Hot as fire ! It will kill the roses.

DELILLE.

I put shades over mine. I tremble while I ask the favor—

CARBONEL, *as before.*

Will you have some wine ?

DELILLE.

No, thank you ! I was about to ask the favor of—

CARBONEL, *as before.*

So you, too, cultivate roses ?

DELILLE.

Yes ! Last year I exhibited the "Standard of Marengo."

CARBONEL.

And I the "Triumph of Avranches," three inches in diameter. Have you it ?

DELILLE.

No. Monsieur, I tremble while I—

CARBONEL, *offering snuff-box.*

Will you take a pinch ?

DELILLE.

No, thank you. I tremble while I ask you for—

CARBONEL, *firmly.*

What ?

DELILLE, *disconcerted.*

For one—who—a graft of the "Triumph."

CARBONEL, *quickly.*

What ! Certainly, my dear young friend, with the greatest pleasure—   [*Going.*

DELILLE.

But, monsieur—

CARBONEL.

I'll put it in moss for you myself.   [*Going.*

DELILLE, *aside.*

He won't stay. [*Aloud*] Monsieur Carbonel—

CARBONEL, *at door.*

With the greatest of pleasure—delighted—
[*Aside*] I got out of that well!   [*Exit at back.*

DELILLE.

He's gone—and I haven't said a word.   Idiot!
beast! fool! ass!

CÉCILE, *entering gayly, at back.*

Well, Monsieur Victor!

DELILLE, *aside, mournfully.*

Now it's her turn!

CÉCILE.

Have you had a talk with papa?

DELILLE.

Yes, mademoiselle—

CÉCILE.

And are you satisfied with your interview?

DELILLE.

Enchanted ! The best proof is that he has gone to fetch what I asked for—

CÉCILE, *naively*.

Then he's looking for me ?

DELILLE.

No, not you ; some grafts of roses.

CÉCILE, *astonished*.

Grafts !

DELILLE.

Yes, mademoiselle—for a quarter of an hour we talked about nothing but roses.

CÉCILE.

But why was that ?

DELILLE.

Because—because I am the victim of a dreadful infirmity—I am timid.

CÉCILE.

You, too ?

DELILLE.

Timid to the verge of idiocy ! Can you believe it ? I could sooner kill myself than utter aloud what I have kept saying to myself these three months past—and that is, that I love you ! that I adore you ! that you are an angel—

CÉCILE.

It seems to me you say that very well.

DELILLE, *astonished at his audacity.*

Have I said anything ? Oh, forgive me ! Don't think of it any more. I didn't mean to—it slipped out—I'll never do it again—I swear—

CÉCILE, *quickly.*

Don't swear ! I do not require an oath ! You, timid, a lawyer ! How do you contrive to plead ?

DELILLE.

I don't. I tried once, and shall never try again.

CÉCILE.

Tell me about it.

DELILLE.

My aunt got me a client. Heaven knows, I never sought him. He was a very passionate man, and had once struck his wife with a stick.

CÉCILE, *reproachfully.*

And you defended the wretch ?

DELILLE.

Wait till you hear *how* I defended him ! The great day came. All my friends were in court. I had prepared a brilliant speech. I knew it by heart. All at once there was an awful silence. The President bowed to me, and said courteously, "Will the counsel proceed?" I rose—I tried to speak—I couldn't utter a sound. Every eye was on me—the President invited me with a gesture to go on—my client called, "Speak! speak!" At last I made an almost superhuman effort—something rattled in my throat—then it seemed to burst, and I stammered out, "Messieurs, I solicit for the accused—the utmost severity of the law." Then I fell back into my seat.

CÉCILE.

And your client?

DELILLE.

Got what I solicited—six months in prison.

CÉCILE.

He deserved them.

DELILLE.

Yes, it was too little for what he made me suffer. I didn't take my fee—it's true he forgot to offer it. And now that you know my infirmity, tell me, how is it possible for me to ask your father for your hand?

CÉCILE.

I can't ask him to give it you.

DELILLE, *naively.*

No, I suppose that wouldn't do. Well, we must wait till aunt gets better.

CÉCILE, *quickly.*

Wait! Don't you know, papa has another offer?

DELILLE, *overwhelmed.*

Another!

CÉCILE.

Yes, and he's here, and he has papa's promise.

DELILLE.

Good gracious! So I have to face a struggle, a rival.

CÉCILE.

But I don't love him; and if I am forced to marry him, I shall die.

DELILLE.

Die! You! [*Boldly*] Where is your father? Send him to me.

CÉCILE.

You will ask him?

DELILLE, *heroically.*

I will!

CÉCILE.

I'll fetch him. [*Going.*] Courage! Courage!
[*Exit at back.*

DELILLE, *alone.*

Yes, I will ask him ; that is, not directly—I'll write.   I write a very *bold hand.*   [*Sitting.*]   This is the thing—a letter does not blush and tremble. [*Writes rapidly as he speaks.*]   I did not know I was so eloquent.   [*Folds and addresses note*] "A Monsieur Carbonel."   [*Unconsciously puts a stamp on.*]   There !   Now it's all right.

CARBONEL, *outside.*

Keep them fresh.   He'll take them soon.

DELILLE, *frightened.*

He, already !   I can't give him this.   Ah, I'll put it in front of the clock.   [*Puts letter before clock and returns C.*]

CARBONEL, *entering at back and coming R.*

My dear friend, your grafts are ready.

DELILLE.

Thank you !   [*Aside*] He has not seen Cécile. [*Aloud*] On the clock.   [*Points.*]

CARBONEL.

What did you say ?

DELILLE.

A letter.   I'll return for the answer.

> [*Exit quickly at back.*

CARBONEL.

On the clock—a letter ! [*He takes it.*]

CÉCILE, *entering L. I. E.*

Oh, papa, I've been looking for you. [*Astonished.*] But where is M. Delille ?

CARBONEL.

Just gone, but it seems he has written to me— on the clock.

CÉCILE.

What ?

CARBONEL.

Yes, it is for me—see, he has put a stamp on. [*Reads*] "Monsieur, I love your daughter ; no, I do not love her—"

CÉCILE.

Eh ?

CARBONEL, *continuing.*

"I adore her—" [*To Cécile*] Go away, you must not hear this !

CÉCILE.

But I know it, papa.

CARBONEL.

Oh, I suppose that makes it all right. [*Reading*] "I adore her." [*Speaking*] How did you know it ?

CÉCILE.

He told me.

4

CARBONEL.

Very improper on his part.

CÉCILE.

Go on ! what else does he say ?

CARBONEL, *reading.*

" You can offer me but two things—her hand or the grave." [*Speaking*] Since he gives me a choice, I'll let him have the grave.

CÉCILE.

Oh, dear papa, when you say you love me so much ! [*Kisses him.*]

CARBONEL, *aside.*

Lucky Delille ! [*Aloud*] But what can I say to Garadoux ?

CÉCILE.

Yes, I see—you're too timid—

CARBONEL.

Timid ! I ! Nonsense ! One man's as good as another.

CÉCILE.

Certainly—if you except Garadoux !

CARBONEL.

I'm not afraid of him, and I know exactly what to say to him. By the way, what ought I to say ?

CÉCILE.

Don't *say* anything; follow M. Delille's example—write.

CARBONEL.

I will. [*Sits.*] Here is a very *firm pen.* [*Writing*] "Dear monsieur—" [*To Cécile*] What next?

CÉCILE, *dictating.*

"Your suit flatters—"

CARBONEL, *writing.*

"And honors me—" [*Speaking*] Let us soften the blow.

CÉCILE, *dictating.*

"But I regret it is impossible to accord you my daughter's hand."

CARBONEL, *writing.*

"Daughter's hand." [*Speaking*] That isn't enough. I must give a reason.

CÉCILE.

I'll give one; go on. [*Dictating*] "I beg you to believe that, in writing this, I only yield with the greatest reluctance to considerations entirely private and personal, which in no way lessen the esteem I shall always entertain for you." [*Speaking*] Now sign!

CARBONEL.

You call that a reason?

CÉCILE.

A diplomatic one; it may mean everything or
nothing.

GARADOUX, *outside.*

Take that to my room.

CARBONEL.

His voice !

CÉCILE.

I leave you.

CARBONEL.

No, don't.   What am I to do with this?
[*Indicating letter.*]

CÉCILE.

Ring for Annette, and bid her give it to M.
Garadoux.   Now, *au revoir*, you dear, good papa.
[*Kisses him, and exit L.*]

CARBONEL.

She's a spoilt child !   Now for Annette !
[*Rings.*]

GARADOUX, *entering at back.*

Well, papa, are you not ready yet ?   We
ought to be at the mayor's now.

CARBONEL.

Yes.   [*Aside*] If that stupid Annette would
but come.   [*Aloud*] While waiting, I have written a very important letter.

GARADOUX, *not listening.*

I'll tell you a secret, but not a word to your daughter.   They have come!

CARBONEL.

Who have come?

GARADOUX.

My presents for her.

CARBONEL, *aside.*

He has bought the presents.

GARADOUX, *polishing his nails.*

You shall see them—they're superb—particularly a pair of bracelets.   [*Aside*] I must have broken that nail, watering.   [*Aloud*] They're blue enamel and gold.

CARBONEL.

Blue and gold !   [*With great effort*] The letter I have just written—

GARADOUX.

I have not forgotten you, papa.   [*Taking box from pocket.*]   A souvenir—a snuff-box.   Style Louis XV., guaranteed.

CARBONEL, *touched.*

Oh, monsieur, my—my dear son-in-law, you are too good.

GARADOUX.

Dear papa, you know how fond I am of you.

CARBONEL.

And I of you. [*Aside*] It's impossible to give such a letter to a man who presents one with such a snuff-box.

GARADOUX.

Twelve o'clock. The mayor will be waiting !

CARBONEL.

In a moment. I must change my cravat.

GARADOUX.

And I my coat. [*Aside*] Devil take that nail !
[*Exit L. 2 E.*

CARBONEL, *alone.*

I couldn't do it. I must tear this up. And the other—he's coming for my answer. [*Looks at letter.*] No address ! and I didn't put any name in the letter. [*Going to table.*] I'll direct it to Delille—Cécile can't marry both—and Garadoux has bought his presents. [*Reads*] "To Monsieur Victor Delille." Now for a stamp. [*Rises.*] And *now* to put it on the clock. [*Places letter on the clock.*]

DELILLE, *entering at back.*

It is only I !

CARBONEL.

On the clock!   [*Exit L. I. E.*

DELILLE, *alone.*

On the clock! Hasn't he read it? [*Takes letter.*] Yes! this is the answer. I scarcely dare open it. [*Reads*] "Dear monsieur: Your suit flatters and honors me—" [*Speaks*] How kind he is! [*Reads*] "But I regret it is impossible to accord you my daughter's hand." [*Falling on chair.*] Refused! I knew it!

CÉCILE, *entering at back.*

Monsieur Victor, have you seen—

DELILLE.

Your father? I have. There is his answer. [*Gives letter.*]

CÉCILE.

What, my letter! This wasn't meant for you!

DELILLE, *pointing at address.*

It's directed to me.

CÉCILE.

This is outrageous. I shall have to attend to this affair myself. I'll let you all see *I* am not timid. Send for a carriage. Quick!

DELILLE.

A carriage! For whom?

CÉCILE.

You'll know by and by.   Go !

DELILLE.

I fly !   [*Aside*] What energy !
> [*Exit quickly at back.*

CÉCILE.

Papa shall not break his word to me like this. [*Takes her shawl and bonnet from a chair at back.*]

CARBONEL, *entering L. I. E.*

I've put on my cravat.   [*Sees Cécile.*]   Where are you going ?

CÉCILE, *tying her bonnet.*

Away !   I leave you for ever !   I am about to immure myself in a convent.

CARBONEL.

Eh !

CÉCILE.

A damp and cold one, where I shall not live long.   But you will not care, for you did not love me enough to save me from a man I hate.

CARBONEL.

But it's impossible !   He's bought his presents. Lovely ones, including a Louis XV. snuff-box for me.

CÉCILE.

So you have sacrificed me to a snuff-box. Farewell, cruel father !

CARBONEL.

It is no sacrifice ! He is a charming young man ; and in the end you will learn to—besides, he's dressing to go to the mayor's.

CÉCILE.

Tell him you can't accompany him: Say you're ill. [*She takes off bonnet and shawl.*]

CARBONEL.

Ah ! that is a good idea ; but he was here five minutes ago.

CÉCILE.

People can die in less time than that. Say it's a rush of blood ! [*Calling*] Annette, hurry, bring papa's dressing-gown !

CARBONEL.

No, no ! I don't want it.

ANNETTE, *entering with dressing-gown.*
What is the matter ?

CÉCILE.

Nothing serious. Bring some *eau sucrée.*
[*Helping Carbonel with gown.*] Put this on !

CARBONEL.

I don't like playing such a part.

CÉCILE.

Never mind ! now the other sleeve !

CARBONEL.

And, look here, I won't say a word. You'll have to manage it all.

CÉCILE.

I know that. [*Making him sit in arm-chair.*] Annette—a foot-stool and a cushion.

ANNETTE, *bringing them.*

Here, mademoiselle.

CÉCILE.

I hear him. [*Takes glass and stands by her father.*]

GARADOUX, *entering with hat.*

Now we're all ready. [*Seeing Carbonel.*] Ah ! what has happened ?

CÉCILE.

Papa has had a sudden—

GARADOUX.

What ?

CÉCILE.

Rush of blood. He is suffering greatly. It

will be impossible for him to go out to-day. Will it not, papa ?

CARBONEL, *aside.*

I protest by my silence.

GARADOUX.

Poor M. Carbonel ! I think it would be well to apply some leeches.

ANNETTE.

Yes, I'll go for some.

CARBONEL.

No, no !

CÉCILE, *quickly.*

This is better for him. [*Gives him glass.*] Drink, papa. [*He drinks.*]

GARADOUX.

It doesn't do to take liberties with one's health. [*Trimming his nails.*] Health is like a fortune—not really appreciated till it's lost.

CARBONEL, *aside.*

I wonder how long I'm to be smothered up here.

CÉCILE, *to Garadoux.*

These attacks of papa's generally last several days ; and if, by chance, your affairs call you to Paris—

GARADOUX.

I couldn't think of leaving M. Carbonel while he is ill.

CARBONEL, *aside.*

An excellent young man !

GARADOUX.

Besides, this need not delay our marriage.   I can go alone to the mayor.

CÉCILE.

Eh ?

GARADOUX.

M. Carbonel's presence is not absolutely necessary.   He can give his consent in writing.

CÉCILE.

Papa is too fatigued now.

GARADOUX.

Oh, it's only a signature. [*Sitting at table.*] I'll write the body.

CÉCILE, *low.*

Don't sign !

GARADOUX, *bringing paper and pen.*

Sign here !

CARBONEL.

But—

CÉCILE.

What shall I do ? [*Takes inkstand and hides it behind her back.*]

CARBONEL.

Where is the inkstand ?

GARADOUX, *after looking on table.*

Mademoiselle is kind enough to hold it for you.

CARBONEL.

Thank you, my dear child. [*He dips pen.*]

CÉCILE, *aside.*

All hope is gone !

DELILLE, *entering running, at back.*

The carriage is at the door.

GARADOUX.

What carriage ?

DELILLE, *astonished.*

What ! Monsieur Garadoux !

GARADOUX, *aside.*

Devilish unfortunate !

DELILLE.

You have been well since—

GARADOUX, *quickly.*

Perfectly !

CARBONEL.

So you know one another ?

DELILLE.

Yes, I had the honor to defend monsieur—he was my first client.

CÉCILE.

Ah ! [*To Carbonel, low*] Imprisoned for six months !

CARBONEL, *rising in consternation.*

What's this ? [*To Garadoux*] You have been in prison ?

GARADOUX.

It was nothing—a quarrel—in a moment of excitement—

CÉCILE.

Monsieur struck his first wife with a stick.

ANNETTE, *coming L. C.*

Oh, the villain ! [*Puts back chair and footstool.*]

CARBONEL.

My poor Cécile ! [*To Garadoux*] Go, sir ! Leave this house, you wife-beater ! Take away your presents. Here is your snuff-box. [*Offers his old horn one.*]

GARADOUX.

Excuse me, that is not the right one.

CARBONEL, *with dignity giving the other*.
There it is !—you may keep the snuff I put in it.

GARADOUX.

I am glad, monsieur, that this little incident has so quickly restored you. [*Going, to Delille*] Idiot !   [*Exit L. 2 E.*

CARBONEL.

What was that he said ?

CÉCILE, *low to Delille*.

Now then, ask him at once. Put on your gloves.

DELILLE.

But isn't it—

CÉCILE.

Don't be afraid. He's more timid than you.

DELILLE, *bravely*.

Oh, he's timid, is he ? [*Begins to put on gloves.*]

CÉCILE, *low to Carbonel*.

He's going to ask for my hand. Put on your gloves.

CARBONEL.

But isn't it—

CÉCILE.

Don't be afraid. He's more timid than you.

CARBONEL, *bravely*.

Oh, he's timid, is he ?   [*Puts on gloves.*]

DELILLE, *boldly*.

Monsieur !

CARBONEL, *same manner*.

Monsieur !

DELILLE, *resolutely*.

For the second time, I ask for your daughter's hand.

CARBONEL.

Monsieur, you ask in a tone—

DELILLE, *sternly*.

It is the tone I choose to use, monsieur.

CARBONEL, *same manner*.

Then I am happy to grant your request, monsieur.

DELILLE.

But you grant it in a tone—

CARBONEL, *sternly*.

It is the tone I choose to use, monsieur.

DELILLE.

Monsieur ! ! !

CARBONEL.

Monsieur ! ! !

CÉCILE, *coming between them.*

[*Aside*] They'll quarrel in a minute. [*Aloud*] Monsieur Victor, papa hopes you will stay to dinner. That was what you wished to say, wasn't it, papa?

CARBONEL.

I suppose so! But mind, he mustn't break any glasses. [*Aside*] I'll make him try the new wine.

CÉCILE.

Oh, I'll answer for him. He has nothing more to be nervous about now. Have you, Victor?

DELILLE.

I am not quite sure about that, Cécile.

CÉCILE.

Do you know, I have never felt nervous till now? [*To the audience*] You have seen these two timid people—well, I am just as timid as they were, and we shall all remain in the same unhappy state, until we receive the assurance of your approval.

5   CURTAIN.

A BAD CASE.

AN ORIGINAL COMEDY IN ONE ACT.

By JULIAN MAGNUS and H. C. BUNNER.

CHARACTERS.

ARTHUR CHISHOLM, M. D., aged 30.

MISS LETITIA DALRYMPLE, aged 50.

MISS SYLVIA DALRYMPLE, *her niece,* aged 19.

LUCY, *a servant.*

SCENE : Smallington Centre, N. Y.

TIME—The Present.

A BAD CASE.

SCENE : Drawing-room in Miss Dalrymple's House. Windows to ground at back, showing distant landscape. Doors R. and L.

Miss Dalrymple and Lucy discovered at rise of curtain.

MISS DALRYMPLE, *bonnet and shawl on.*
Lucy, I am obliged to go out for an hour—

LUCY.

What, ma'am, with your bad elbow, and you expecting your nephew every minute ? After sending for the new doctor, too ?

MISS DALRYMPLE.

New doctor indeed ! I wish old Jenkins hadn't died—though to be sure for the last twenty years he never gave anything but syrup of squills, for fear he should make a mistake, and he was so shaky that when he counted my pulse he always made it one hundred and fifty. It's two hours

since I sent for this new doctor, and he hasn't
come yet. My elbow might have died in half the
time. I mean I might have died. What is this
new doctor like ?

LUCY.

I don't know, ma'am ; he only came day before
yesterday ; but I have heard he is young and good-
looking, and they say there's been quite an epi-
demic among the single ladies this morning.
But must you go out, ma'am ?

MISS DALRYMPLE.

Yes, Lucy. The *creatures*—I can't call them
anything else—no sooner heard that my elbow was
troubling me than they called a meeting to elect
that Mrs. Smith Presidentess. I am not going to
let them beat me like that. No ; if I wasn't
strong enough to walk there, I'd crawl, even if
I had to be carried on a shutter. And when the
conspirators meet they will find me among them—
the Nemesis of Smallington Centre !

LUCY.

But if your nephew, Mr. Blackhurst, should
arrive while you're a Nemesising it, ma'am ?

MISS DALRYMPLE.

I don't think he will ; there's no fast train
now from New York till the afternoon; and if Mr.
Arthur's anything like what he was eight years ago

when he went away, a slow train won't suit him.
But call Miss Sylvia, and I'll tell her what to do
in case he should come ; and be sure not to say
anything to her about my having had the rheumatism this morning. I don't want to frighten her.
[*Lucy goes toward door as Sylvia enters R.*] I
was just going to call you, miss.

[*Exit Lucy R.*

SYLVIA.

Did you want me, aunt ?

MISS DALRYMPLE.

Yes, my dear. I have to go out; there are
traitors in our camp. I must make a martyr of
myself, or the Dorcas Society will be wrecked—yes,
wrecked, by that awful, designing Mrs. Smith ! A
widow indeed ! I should like to know where her
husband is.

SYLVIA.

Probably dead !

MISS DALRYMPLE.

I don't believe it, though to be sure she's
enough to have killed any one. What do you
think—she actually proposed to admit gentlemen
to the Society's Tuesday evenings !

SYLVIA.

Horrible !

MISS DALRYMPLE.

Wasn't it ? Now, dear, if by any chance my

nephew should come while I am away, try to make
him comfortable. Treat him as I myself would.
I hear he has quite reformed. And you know he's
my only relation except you. And let me tell
you of a little idea I have in my head. If only
he should like you, and you should like him—
why, can you guess what might happen then ?

SYLVIA.

Like would cure like, I suppose—truth of the
homœopathic principle once more asserted.

MISS DALRYMPLE.

I don't believe in infinitesimal doses.

SYLVIA.

No more do I. [*Aside*] Especially of love.

MISS DALRYMPLE.

You've never seen him, of course, my dear,
but I don't know, really, whether that isn't rather
an advantage ; you'll be all the more predisposed
to like him.

SYLVIA.

I'll do my best, aunty dear.

MISS DALRYMPLE.

You'll have very little difficulty, my love.
You'll be surprised in him—you'll find him quite
a striking young person. A little flighty in his
conversation, perhaps, but—

SYLVIA.

Oh, I like vivacity, aunty.

MISS DALRYMPLE.

Then I'm sure you'll get along very well with my nephew. Good-by, my dear. The machinations of *that* Mrs. Smith demand my attention. Now, don't fail to receive your cousin kindly— avoid any appearance of cold reserve, and don't be astonished if he's a little odd and—foreign in his conversation. Good-by.

[*Exit Miss Dalrymple L.*

SYLVIA, *alone.*

I'm sure I shall never know what to do with him, if he should come. It is horribly awkward —to be left to receive a strange cousin—all alone. What shall I call him ? I can't say " cousin " ; it sounds too familiar. And then—if he's a forward young man. . . . And what am I to talk to him about ? I can't awaken reminiscences of his youth, that's clear. And I daren't talk about his foreign travel. I don't see, though, why I should bother myself so much about him. Aunt Dalrymple's scapegrace nephew, indeed ! A pretty person ! I shouldn't care to see him if there weren't another man in the place—and there *are* other men in the place. There's the clergyman's eldest son just getting to be twenty-one and quite nice ; and the new doctor who came day before yesterday, and the

girls all say he's perfectly sweet. I shan't worry
much over Mr. Blackhurst. I do not propose to
make the slightest preparation for him. I'll receive
him just as I am, and *he* may start the conversation. [*Bell rings.*] The bell! There he is!
And I'm sure I look horrid. [*Runs to mirror
and arranges ribbons.*] Oh, dear, that'll never
do. I'll just run up stairs for a moment.

[*Exit Sylvia, R.*
Enter Lucy L., showing in Chisholm.

CHISHOLM.

Here I am at last! I suppose you thought I'd
never get here!

LUCY.

Miss Dalrymple has been expecting you a long
time, sir.

CHISHOLM.

I'm very sorry to have kept her waiting. Take
her my card. [*Aside*] I don't see why a doctor
shouldn't carry a card, as well as any one else—
especially when it's his first visit. And I'm sure
I had a card somewhere about me. [*Feeling in
pockets*] Ah! here it is! [*Gives it.*

LUCY, *going R.*

Yes, sir! [*Reads*] Mr. Arthur Blackhurst.
[*Aside*] So he's come at last. And he doesn't
look so very scapegrace-y either. [*Aloud*] I'm
so glad you've come, sir!   [*Exit R.*

CHISHOLM, *alone.*

So glad—wonder whether *she* wants me, too. Of all the towns for sick single women, this is the worst —I mean the best. It's business for me, if it is . . . . sentiment for them. I've had only one male patient to-day—but I'm bound to say he occupied more time than even the worst old maid on my list. Let me see, what was his name. He did give me a card. [*Feels for it*] I suppose I must have left it at the house. I'd have been here two hours ago, to attend to this unfortunate elbow, if it hadn't been for him. A very neat black eye he had—a very artistic little mouse. Got it in a fight with a bar-keeper, and wanted it toned down before he could go to see his maiden aunt. I painted it over in distemper—magnesia and honey —and he's drying off now. Ah, now for the next old tabby. [*Sylvia enters R.*] Tabby! why, she's a kitten, bless her!

SYLVIA, *rushing to him.*

Oh, I'm *so* glad you've come! [*Taking both his hands.*

CHISHOLM.

Thank you — you're very kind. [*Aside*] Well, I'm glad I *have* come. [*Aloud*] You see I've only just—

SYLVIA.

Yes, we know you've only just arrived. We had expected you a little earlier; but we won't reproach you now you are here. Sit down, do [*they sit, C. and L. C.*]. You must make yourself quite at home, you know.

CHISHOLM.

I'll try to. [*Aside*] Nice cordial style about the people here!

SYLVIA.

My aunt has been so anxious to see you.

CHISHOLM, *aside*.

Her aunt, too. Wonder what's the matter with the aunt. Confound the aunt!

SYLVIA.

I hope you're quite well. [*Aside*] He seems to feel a little strange. I must be more cordial. [*Aloud*] *Quite* well?

CHISHOLM.

Quite well, thanks. [*Suddenly*] How's your elbow?

SYLVIA.

My elbow! [*Aside*] He *is* very flighty. Perhaps that's a foreign idiom.

CHISHOLM, *embarrassed*.

I mean—I mean—I mean—heavy rain yesterday—bad weather for rheumatism.

SYLVIA.

And bad for the corn, too.

CHISHOLM.

The corn! Well, to tell you frankly, corns are not exactly in my line.

SYLVIA, *aside.*

He has no inclination for an agricultural life. I'm afraid he's not thoroughly reformed. Perhaps he has not sown *all* his wild oats. [*Aloud*] Now tell me all about yourself. You don't know how much interest I take in you. What have you been doing the last eight years?

CHISHOLM, *astonished and embarrassed.*

Well—that is—you see—

SYLVIA, *quietly.*

Oh! I beg your pardon—I ought not to have asked that, for I suppose you have been very—very—[*hesitates.*

CHISHOLM.

Well, I have been rather—rather—[*hesitates.*

SYLVIA.

Yes, of course, but that is all over now, and you're going to settle down here and be quite proper and steady, aren't you?

CHISHOLM.

Yes, certainly, Miss Dalrymple. [*Aside*] It's nice to have a pretty girl show so much interest in one.

SYLVIA.

Oh, you needn't be so formal. I feel already as though we were very old friends.

CHISHOLM.

Thank you ! [*Aside*] I wish she'd begin about her elbow; she didn't seem to like my referring to it.

SYLVIA.

Now, I don't know what to call you. I can't address you as Mister, it seems so distant and unfriendly toward one of whom I am going to see so much.

CHISHOLM.

I hope so.

SYLVIA.

Oh yes, indeed. Now we have you here, we're not going to let you slip away in a hurry. We'll not allow you to fall back again into—rather—rather—you know.

CHISHOLM.

I don't want to. I think it's very nice here. [*Change of tone*] Your elbow's better, I suppose ?

SYLVIA, *aside.*

What a queer phrase that is ! I wonder what it

means? It won't do to appear too innocent. [*Aloud*] Oh yes, thank you.

CHISHOLM, *aside.*

She needn't thank *me.* She's getting well too soon. She's very pretty. What an interesting invalid she'd make! [*Aloud*] I think all you need is toning up.

SYLVIA.

And I've heard that all you need is toning *down.*

CHISHOLM.

At least our two tones seem likely to be harmonious.

SYLVIA.

Why should they not, Ar—Arthur?

CHISHOLM.

Arthur? [*Rapidly moving his chair up to hers*] Miss Dalrymple!

SYLVIA.

You may call me Sylvia.

CHISHOLM.

You are only too good. [*Seizing her hand, speaking hurriedly*] Ah! if you could but know what an instantaneous impression your beauty, your grace, your delicacy have made upon me, you would not wonder, Winona—

SYLVIA.

Sylvia, you mean !

CHISHOLM, *as before.*

Sylvia, I mean—you would not wonder that this young heart yearns toward you, in all its—its —its adolescent efflorescence, Miranda—

SYLVIA.

But my name is *not* Miranda !

CHISHOLM.

Of course not. [*Sinking on his knee*] Ophelia, I can no longer restrain the throbbings of a heart that—

SYLVIA.

Oh hush, Arthur !   You must not speak to me like that—at least, not until you have seen my aunt—*our* aunt.

CHISHOLM [*rising, startled*].

Our aunt ! [*Aside*] Look here, this is getting a little too rapid for me. [*Resuming his professional air*] I trust your elbow is entirely well ?

SYLVIA, *aside.*

That elbow again ! Oh, gracious me ! I do believe—upon my word—the poor fellow—he's just a little—crazy, you know.   The hot climates—or something—have turned his head.   And [*looking out window*] there is aunt coming. [*Aloud*] Arthur, aunty's coming.

CHISHOLM.

The deuce she is !

SYLVIA.

Yes. Aren't you glad to see her ?

CHISHOLM.

Well, no, not particularly.

SYLVIA.

Not glad to see aunty ?

CHISHOLM.

I wish "aunty" was in—Afghanistan.

SYLVIA.

O Arthur ! [*Aside*] He's really crazy. I must humor him. [*Aloud*] Well, suppose we go into the library.

CHISHOLM.

Are *you* coming ?

SYLVIA.

Yes. Then you'll feel more like seeing aunty.

CHISHOLM.

Perhaps I shall. Come along, by all means.

6

SYLVIA, *leading him R.*

You go. I'll follow in a moment. [*Chisholm enters room. Sylvia immediately shuts and locks door.*] He's quite crazy, poor fellow. I am afraid he'll do aunty some mischief. However, he's safe there for a few minutes, and I can send for the gardener to help control him.

MISS DALRYMPLE, *entering L.*

Of all the disgraceful outrages ever perpetrated, this last outbreak of my wretched nephew's is the worst! [*Sinks into chair.*

SYLVIA.

What has he done, aunt?

MISS DALRYMPLE.

Done! What hasn't he done? Broke into the Dorcas rooms, just as I was about to overwhelm that Smith woman, with a dreadful black eye and very drunk, and, seizing me round the waist, tried to make me dance, while she laughed her horrible, vulgar laugh and secured nearly all the votes!

SYLVIA.

You must forgive him, aunt. He is not accountable for his actions.

MISS DALRYMPLE.

I hear he has been in the town for hours--

that he had a fight in a low saloon, where he got that terrible eye.

SYLVIA.

I didn't notice anything the matter with his eye.

MISS DALRYMPLE.

Has he been here then ?

SYLVIA.

Yes. I've locked him up in that room.

CHISHOLM, *pounding on door.*

Sylvia ! let me out. I'm not afraid of your aunt. She's nothing to me.

MISS DALRYMPLE.

Listen to that—the ungrateful boy, for whom I have done so much.

SYLVIA.

I am sure I tried all in my power to keep him quiet and happy.

MISS DALRYMPLE.

Yes, dear, I am sure you did ; the mischief was done before he saw you. [*Chisholm pounds on door.*

SYLVIA.

Shall I risk letting him out ?

MISS DALRYMPLE.

Call Lucy and the gardener first. He may be dangerous in this state.

SYLVIA.

But they mustn't hurt him.

MISS DALRYMPLE.

Hurt him! I'll have him taken at once to the police-station. [*Chisholm pounds.*] Yes, sir. My gardener and my maid shall take you to the police-station.

CHISHOLM.

I'll smash your gardener and your maid and the whole family if I get a chance at you.

MISS DALRYMPLE.

Hear the wretch!

LUCY, *entering L.*

O marm! O Miss Dalrymple! What is all this horrible noise?

MISS DALRYMPLE.

Lucy, where's the gardener?

LUCY.

He's out, marm, for the day. You gave him permission this morning.

MISS DALRYMPLE.

Then how shall we get rid of this drunken wretch ?

SYLVIA.

O aunty, he's not drunk !

MISS DALRYMPLE.

What is he, then ?

SYLVIA.

He's only crazy, aunty, dear—only the least bit insane. [*Chisholm pounds ferociously.*] He's only a little bit flighty and foreign in his ways. But I'm not afraid of him. I'll open the door.

LUCY.

Oh, law ! miss, don't go near him. It may be contiguous.

SYLVIA.

Oh, he was really quite nice and calm with me.

MISS DALRYMPLE.

Yes, open the door, Sylvia ; and I myself will lead the miscreant to the tribunal of justice.

LUCY.

She means the police-station, where the green lamp is. O marm, don't be so hard on him.

SYLVIA.

O aunty, spare him ! [*Kneeling.*] He's really so very nice.

Lucy, *sobbing.*

So very nice, ma'am. Oh! [*She starts, as Chisholm batters on door.*

MISS DALRYMPLE.

Sylvia, rise, I command you, and bring forth the culprit. [*Sylvia opens door.*] Come out, sir! [*Pause.*

LUCY.

Please come out, sir. [*Pause.*

SYLVIA.

Please come out—Arthur—dear!

CHISHOLM, *entering.*

What the—dickens do you mean by locking me in there? Have I fallen into a mad-house?

MISS DALRYMPLE.

Sylvia! What does this mean? Who is this man you have been concealing in my house?

LUCY.

Yes, Miss Sylvia, what is this clandestineness?

SYLVIA, *to Miss Dalrymple.*

Is not this your nephew?

MISS DALRYMPLE.

No!!

SYLVIA, *to Chisholm.*

Are you not Arthur?

CHISHOLM.

That is my name. [*To Miss Dalrymple*] Madam, I entered your house upon a perfectly honorable errand, and strictly in pursuance of my profession.

MISS DALRYMPLE.

Young man, if you're in the Electro-plating, History of the Bible, Sewing Machine, or Lightning-rod line, I don't want any of them.

CHISHOLM.

Madam, when I came here, I sent up my card.

LUCY.

Yes, I took it to Miss Sylvia; it read as plain as print, "Mr. Arthur Blackhurst."

CHISHOLM.

The man whose eye I painted this morning! You must excuse me; I had his card in my pocket and forgot to look at it. I am Dr. Arthur Chisholm.

SYLVIA.

Arthur Chisholm!

MISS DALRYMPLE.

Dr. Chisholm!

LUCY.

The new physicianer!

CHISHOLM.

Precisely—who has spent a most agreeable half hour with this young lady.

SYLVIA.

I am afraid it was a great deal too agreeable. Oh dear!

MISS DALRYMPLE.

Never mind, my love. I'm sure the doctor will forgive you if you've been rude to him.

SYLVIA.

But I wasn't rude to him—and that's just what's so *horrible!*

MISS DALRYMPLE.

You will join us at dinner to-day, Dr. Chisholm, and permit us to make our apologies more fully.

CHISHOLM.

I shall be most happy; and then I shall be able to diagnose more carefully the case of my interesting patient here. [*Indicating Sylvia.*

MISS DALRYMPLE.

But it was I who sent for you, Doctor.

CHISHOLM.

You! Then it was you who had the rheumatism! How's your elbow?

[QUICK CURTAIN.]

COURTSHIP WITH VARIATIONS.

COMEDY IN ONE ACT.

By H. C. BUNNER.

CHARACTERS.

ERNEST ARCHIBALD.

VIRGINIA BERKELEY, *a young widow, his cousin.*

[The French original of this play is "*Le Monde Renversé,*" written by M. Henri de Bornier.]

COURTSHIP WITH VARIATIONS.

SCENE: A drawing-room in a country house, prettily furnished. Door from hall, R. 2 E. Door to next room, L. U. E. Through large French windows at the back is seen a flower-garden; in the distance, a view of the Hudson. Large table a little to the left of C., with a chair on each side. Jardinière, with flowers, in the window R. Mantelpiece at L. 1 E.

ERNEST ARCHIBALD stands by the mantelpiece, looking rather mournfully at a photograph in a velvet frame. He sighs in a mild and subdued way, and his inspection appears to yield him but a limited amount of satisfaction. After a moment, however, he breaks the silence and opens the play by soliloquizing:

If I dared! But I don't dare. I didn't dare before the advent of the late-lamented Berkeley; and now that he has come and gone, I don't see any material improvement in the position. If she was formidable as a girl, she's only doubly terrifying as a widow. O Cousin Virginia! Cousin Virginia!—hello, Cousin Virginia!

The tone of his sentimental apostrophe suddenly changes, and his last repetition of the name is simply a surprised saluta- tion, addressed to a young lady who has just entered the room R. 2 E.   The young lady has bright eyes and an air of entire self-possession, which, in conjunction with a mischievous smile, give a faint hint of the reason why Ernest hadn't dared.   And the general appearance of the young lady sufficiently explains why he felt badly about it.   VIRGINIA BERKELEY carries on her arm a traveling-shawl, and in her hand an extremely small work-basket, of which luggage her host proceeds to disembar- rass her.

ERNEST.

Why, my dear Virginia, we didn't expect you so soon ! Let me take your shawl—and that work-basket.   How did you get here ?

VIRGINIA.

Ernest, where's my aunt ?

ERNEST.

She's gone to the station to meet you.

VIRGINIA.

What ! did she think I was going to take that hot, stuffy railroad to ride twenty miles ? As you would say, not much ! I drove up from Peekskill in the phaeton.   John is putting my pony in the stable at this moment.   Pony's tired—which re- minds me that I am too.   But you don't offer me a chair.   You stand still and look at me, just as you've done for twenty years, ever since we were small children in pinafores.   Your pinafore was dirty : mine was clean. You used to stare at me then : you do now. I don't see that it has ever done you any good. It is very complimentary, but I should prefer a chair.

ERNEST.

I don't know why you want a chair when I am present. You always sit down on—

VIRGINIA, *severely.*

Ernest ! No slang, if you please ! Especially, no impertinent slang. Ah, thank you ! You have picked out the only uncomfortable chair in the room, but never mind—it will do.

ERNEST.

Virginia, how long are you going to stay here ?

VIRGINIA, *promptly.*

One week. But, if the prospect alarms you already, you may go somewhere else. Well, why are you looking at me now ?

ERNEST.

I'm not looking at you.

VIRGINIA.

What are you looking at, then ?

ERNEST, *hesitatingly.*

I'm looking at your dress.

VIRGINIA, *absently*.

Oh, yes. I've left off my mourning.

ERNEST, *involuntarily*.

Hop-là !

VIRGINIA.

Ernest ! What do you mean by that extraordinary remark—to characterize it mildly ? It is the first sign of animation you have given. I have no objection to vivacity, but the form it takes is a little peculiar.

ERNEST.

Now look here, Virginia ; you didn't care a copper for him, either.

VIRGINIA.

Whom do you mean—what do you mean—are you insane, Ernest ?

ERNEST.

I mean the late-lamented. Oh, don't look indignant and offended. It was your mother's marriage ; not yours. I don't say anything disrespectful of the late Berkeley—no, far from it. I've had a high regard for him ever since he died and left you your freedom and his fortune and a pony-phaeton. But, alive, he was a decided bore !

VIRGINIA.

Ernest !

ERNEST.

Yes, a bore ! He bored *me !*

VIRGINIA.

You ? .

ERNEST.

Yes ! For—because—you know.

VIRGINIA.

Great heavens, Ernest ! it isn't possible that you're trying to make love to me !

ERNEST, *somewhat taken aback.*

Isn't it ?

VIRGINIA.

How long since you got that idea into your head ?

ERNEST.

Well, I didn't quite expect this kind of thing —at least, so much of it. I meant to tell you that—that—for a long time I've been—

VIRGINIA.

Well, what ?

ERNEST.

Er—er—sighing—

VIRGINIA, *highly amused.*

Sighing ? *Sighing ?* Oh, ha-ha-ha-ha-ha ! Sighing ? O Ernest, dear ; *do* tell me next time you sigh—I should *so* like to see you sighing. [*Continuation of ha-ha's.*]

ERNEST.

Oh, confound it ! Virginia ! don't laugh so. Let me speak.

VIRGINIA.

Certainly—oh, certainly. I'd like to see how you do it. Take care ! you're not the first, you know. If you don't introduce some novel effect into your courtship, you've no chance at all. Come, let's hear you sigh.

ERNEST, *confidentially, to vacancy.*

Not the first. I should think not ! Perhaps this would be a good situation to exit on.

VIRGINIA.

Proceed. Sigh !

ERNEST.

Well, then—I love you !

VIRGINIA.

Doubtless. Proceed.

ERNEST.

I—I—adore you.

VIRGINIA.

Couldn't you adore me with a little variation of style ?

ERNEST.

If you doubt that my love will last—

VIRGINIA.

I don't. That's just what I'm afraid of. It's a very stupid kind of love.

ERNEST.

But I ask so little, Virginia. I don't demand that you should love me—

VIRGINIA.

Now, that is really kind and considerate of you!

ERNEST.

When you left this house two years ago, Virginia, you were not so cruel to me. I was twenty years old—it was spring—and that was the last day of spring on which you left us. Do you not remember that time, my cousin? Has the odor of your ball-bouquets overpowered the perfume of our woodland flowers? *I* have not forgotten, at least. I can see you now: running down the long walks of the garden; your dark hair flying behind you; I can hear the clear ring of your voice as you called my name. Ah, what a grand air you had then; though you were only a little girl just from boarding-school. I was sometimes almost afraid of you, but I always admired you— ay! I loved you, though I did not know it.

VIRGINIA.

You were better off then than you are now.

7

ERNEST.

I was! for you were kinder. Those were the days when you used to say : " Cousin Ernest, come and make love to me ! " You don't say that any more, now.

VIRGINIA.

I do not. But come, my poor Ernest, what folly this is ! If you would only stop loving me, I should like you so much better. Affection doesn't improve your personal appearance, my dear. You make most horrid faces to accompany your compliments. Seriously, though, you are spoiling my visit for me. I came here to have a good time ; to see you and my aunt ; and no sooner have I arrived than you begin talking to me in this disagreeable way. You must not make love to me. We are very good friends ; I love you as a cousin. Love, Ernest ! Why, it's like taking a newspaper—I might discontinue my subscription at any time. But friendship—it is a precious book, that we read and re-read a hundred times, and never grow tired of. Why should we try to force our inclinations ? The love we seek would spoil that which we now enjoy. Come, you will be a good boy, and obey me.

ERNEST, *with promptitude and decision.*

I will not.

VIRGINIA, *surprised.*

What?

ERNEST.

I mean, I *can* not. I love you, and—

VIRGINIA.

Then I'll go back to Peekskill instanter.

ERNEST.

You can't. I saw your coachman pass the window just this moment. He is undoubtedly gone to the tavern, which is half a mile down the road.

VIRGINIA.

Then, if I've got to stay, we'll settle this at once. I hate you. I detest you. I shall always continue to hate and detest you !

ERNEST.

Virginia—cousin !

VIRGINIA, *not at all mollified.*

Don't come near me.

ERNEST.

But—

VIRGINIA.

No !

She arises, walks swiftly to the mirror, and removes her hat, which, being of the Gainsborough pattern, lends a rakish air to the wearer. Its removal enables her to look consistently languid, and she throws herself into a large arm-chair to the right of the table, and tries to pose for a martyr. The unfortunate ERNEST pauses in a moody promenade from end to end of the room, and turns to address her. Immediate resumption of hostilities.

ERNEST.

Look here, Virginia.

VIRGINIA.

I will not look there, sir. I am your victim. Don't speak to me. You've put me all out of sorts.

ERNEST, *on the left of the table.*

You must hear me ! My life is at your feet—

VIRGINIA looks down at the tiny tip of her shoe, resting comfortably on a brioche, as if to verify the assertion. Her lover, however, refuses to take any notice of this small outrage, and proceeds :

I will make you the tenderest of husbands—

VIRGINIA, *starting to her feet in horror.*

Husbands ! The audacity of the wretch !

ERNEST.

Well, suppose—

VIRGINIA, *tragically pacing the room.*

Leave me, sir ! I will bear this no longer.

ERNEST.

At least, pardon me if I—

VIRGINIA.

There's no *if* about it. You have. But I will not pardon you.

ERNEST, *immovable.*

What a fool I've been! Oh—there, there— I'm going. You see I'm going.

VIRGINIA, *unable to see anything of the sort.*

Then what are you stopping there for ?

ERNEST, *frankly.*

To look at you. You are so deucedly pretty that way.

Upon this he prudently retires through the left upper doorway just as VIRGINIA returns to her arm-chair. Left alone, the young lady laughs quietly to herself for a moment, and then looks serious. Her cheeks flush, apparently with indignation, and she indulges in a brief and fragmentary soliloquy.

VIRGINIA.

The wretch! [*With satisfaction*] I did well to laugh at him. [*With a slight touch of compunction*] Perhaps I laughed a little too much. [*With an air of judicial abstraction*] For, after all, he couldn't help it. [*Softening*] Poor Ernest! [*Quite melted*] Poor dear!

The left upper door softly opens, and the head of the exile appears. This movement seems to be inopportune on his part, for, as soon as his cousin perceives it, her face clouds over

again. The unwelcome youth enters, however, and advances
to the fray. His reception is not encouraging.

VIRGINIA.

Ernest! You back?

ERNEST, *with resolute cheerfulness.*

Yes. You see. Come, don't be so tragic.
I generally go when I'm boun—I mean, when
I'm sent away. I went when you told me to. I
saw it was best. Anger sat enthroned upon your
bang. I went out on the lawn, and I hadn't
taken two steps before up flew a little bird—yes,
a little bird! He flew first right, and then left,
and then he whistled three times. If that wasn't
an omen, I don't know what is. It was an omen.
And in obedience to it I return.

VIRGINIA, *puzzled.*

But I don't understand—

ERNEST.

Oh, but I do. That little bird didn't whistle
for nothing. He meant to say to me: "Look
here, you're a nice sort of a fellow, to give it up
like this! Because your cousin frowns and tells
you to leave her when you say you love her, you
quietly put on your hat and go! Bah! that's the
kind of thing you must expect in love. Go back
and begin again. Go on worse than ever. She
expects you—"

VIRGINIA, *indignantly.*

She does not!

ERNEST, *undisturbed.*

I'm only telling you what the bird said. Talk to *him.* "Go back, old fellow," he went on, "and try it again." So I'm back. Charge it to the dickey-bird.

VIRGINIA.

And you think your bird and your impudence will have any effect on me?

ERNEST, *placidly.*

Can't say. Hope so.

VIRGINIA, *rising with a nervous start.*

Ernest! you'll drive me crazy—no, you won't —you'll make me cry! Oh, dear! Why, Ernest —just put yourself in my place.

ERNEST.

In your place?

VIRGINIA.

Yes—no, that is. I don't mean literally— that would be funny. Courtship with variations.

ERNEST, *meditatively.*

In your place!

VIRGINIA.

Well, yes! In my place. And then perhaps you'd find out, sir, that adoration may be torture

to a woman.   Of what do you suppose my heart
is made, if you think I enjoy having you batter
at its portal in this fashion ?   [*She crosses L.*]

ERNEST.

I suppose it's made of some pretty tough material.

VIRGINIA.

You do ?   Well, come, we'll see how you like
it yourself.   I'm going to convince you—this in-
stant.   It is I who will make love to *you.*   [*She
comes back to the table.*]

ERNEST.

Good joke.

VIRGINIA.

You think so, do you ?   Well, you'll see.   I
am going to pay court to you from now to sun-
down, without pity or remorse.   You shall be the
lady fair, and I the enamored knight.   And take
care of yourself, my lady !

ERNEST.

Good *idea.*

VIRGINIA.

Yes, but—one thing.   I want to gain some
substantial results by this operation.

ERNEST.

If you go about your business properly, you'll
gain *me.*   I'm a pretty substantial result.

VIRGINIA, *seating herself on the left of table.*

Nonsense ! But see—the game is to close at dinner-time—at six o'clock. And from that time to the end of my visit here, you are not to say one single word of love to me. Do you promise ?

ERNEST.

Yes—unless—

VIRGINIA.

Unless ?

ERNEST.

Unless you ask me to.

VIRGINIA, *with sarcastic merriment.*

I accept *that* condition. Unless I ask you to. Well, then—oh, one word more ! You—

ERNEST.

Well ?

VIRGINIA.

You won't take any unfair advantage of your position ?

ERNEST.

Certainly not.

VIRGINIA.

I mean—don't introduce me to any type of lady that I haven't met before.

ERNEST, *emphatically.*

I won't. Don't be afraid. I'll take *you* for a model.

VIRGINIA.

Ladies don't pay compliments, sir! This won't do. We must have a-forfeit. Every time you forget your rôle of lady fair, you shall pay me—let us see—what have you in your pockets?

ERNEST.

Here are ten silver dollars.

VIRGINIA.

Do you want them?

ERNEST.

No, glad to get rid of them.

VIRGINIA.

Well, then, each time that you forget yourself, you shall pay me one of these; proceeds to be devoted to the Home for Indigent and Venerable Females at Peekskill. I'm one of the directors. There are ten "lady directors" of the Home, and some day we expect to get an Indigent and Venerable Female to put in it. So these are your forfeits.

ERNEST.

All right. But what's sauce for an Indigent and Venerable Female is sauce for a young and lovely one. What are you to forfeit to me if you forget that you are a gentleman?

VIRGINIA.

Well, what ?   What do you suggest ?

ERNEST.

Hm !   Say—say, for instance, a kiss—

VIRGINIA, *energetically negative.*

No ! no ! no ! *no !*

ERNEST.

Why not ?

VIRGINIA.

Do you estimate a kiss from me at one dollar only ?

ERNEST.

By no means.   Its value is not to be esti-mated.   I don't even attempt it.   The dollar is merely a counter—an arbitrary representative of value.   But if you are talking on a business basis, I know an old woman who could be induced to go to your Home.   I'll throw her in.   Does that satisfy you ?

VIRGINIA.

No !

ERNEST.

All right then.   The fight is declared off, and the treaty abrogated.   I shall return to my la-bors.

VIRGINIA.

Oh, dear, no !   I can't have that.   And, any-

way—there can't be any danger. I can rely on
myself, on my skill, and my—

ERNEST.

Charms.

VIRGINIA.

A compliment ! Pay me a forfeit.

ERNEST.

Time's not called yet.

VIRGINIA.

Never mind. I don't want to bankrupt you
so soon. You'll lose your silver counters soon
enough. But now—it's all understood, is it ?
The play is cast—we know our rôles ? Then up
goes the curtain. [*She touches a bell on the table.*] Now, then, let the company remember
their cues. [*Rising and bowing to an imaginary
public.*] Ladies and gentlemen, " Courtship with
Variations," comedy in one act, by a collabora-
tion.

And she reseats herself. The exponent of the opposing
rôle takes the chair on the other [R.] side of the table, and
for a silent minute or two both appear to be absorbed in re-
flection. It is the truce before the battle. After another
moment, ERNEST steals a sly glance at his antagonist, and
surprises her in the act of doing the same thing. After this,
there is more silence, and considerable fidgeting in both chairs.
At last VIRGINIA whispers to herself, by way of relief:

He's got to speak, some time or other.

He, however, does not seem to think so. Struck by a sudden idea, he reaches for the diminutive work-basket on the table, and placidly begins a wild travesty of crocheting. The owner of the basket looks on the ruin of her handiwork with some dissatisfaction, but does not venture to interfere. She once more takes refuge in soliloquy:

Ten counters—ten kisses—it's too much, by nine, at least. I've got to do something. Come, to work!

And with a desperate effort she rises and marches around behind the table, to the calm artist in crochet, who raises his eyes languidly and continues to tangle her worsted. She addresses him:

VIRGINIA.

Cousin, are you very clever?

ERNEST, *languidly crocheting.*

Ra-ather!

VIRGINIA.

Not exceptionally so, I suppose?

ERNEST.

Not more so than—[*his eye falls on his counters*]—most people.

VIRGINIA, *leaning over the back of his chair.*

Well, if you're clever at all, tell me why it is I am happy just at this very moment.

ERNEST, *femininely bored.*

Oh, *dear!* I'm *sure* I don't know.

VIRGINIA.

You don't! Well, I'll tell you. I'm happy because I have an opportunity of telling you that there are two things about you that I have always admired—your eyes.

ERNEST, *in a quiet aside.*

Guying, is she?

VIRGINIA.

Let me lift your hair off your forehead—so! Ah! you look well so. Fine forehead, well-arched brows—how is it I never noticed them before? Nose—straight. Greek type.

ERNEST.

These are what you call compliments, I suppose?

VIRGINIA.

I'm always particular in the matter of noses. Let's see. Chin—quite correct. Cheek-bones—not too high and not too low.

ERNEST.

Sounds like a description for the benefit of the police.

VIRGINIA.

And your hand—quite a lady's hand. Long and slender—and dimples, too; upon my word, dimples! [*Aside*] Oh, it's no use.

For this broadside of compliments proves a dead failure. The victim lies back in his chair and plies his crochet-needles, complacently smiling. So far, he seemingly enjoys being wooed. VIRGINIA sits down on the extreme left and meditates. Her eye lights on the jardinière in the window, and it supplies her with an idea. She rises, crosses to the right-hand upper corner, and plucks a rose.

ERNEST, *suddenly and ferociously.*

Yow-oo-oo !

VIRGINIA, *at the jardinière.*

What's the matter ?

ERNEST.

I've stuck your inf—I mean your crochet-needle into my hand.

VIRGINIA, *unmoved by the catastrophe.*

Never mind, dear ; go on crocheting.

ERNEST, *aside.*

Damn crocheting !

VIRGINIA, *crossing back to him.*

Let me put this in your buttonhole, cousin, there !—ah, no ; that's a little too red. We'll tone it down. [*Crossing again to jardinière and back.*] Here's a tuberose. Ah ! now you are—ravishing ! You are a picture ! [*Standing off to admire him.*]

ERNEST.

I'm a daisy, am I?

VIRGINIA.

You are—oh! *what* a daisy you are! [*Clasping her hands.*]

ERNEST, *aside.*

Guying again! Let us resume the offensive. [*Aloud*] Oh, dear!

VIRGINIA.

What is it now?

ERNEST, *spilling the work-basket.*

I don't know—I feel—so—oh!

VIRGINIA.

So what?

ERNEST.

Oh, you've put me all out of sorts! I feel— hysterical!

VIRGINIA, *to herself.*

He's making fun of *me.*

ERNEST, *feebly.*

O cousin! *Please*—send for a doctor.

VIRGINIA, *with masculine indifference.*

Nonsense, my dear child; you'll get over it— you'll get over it.

ERNEST, *plaintively*.

Indeed, I won't. I feel worse now.

VIRGINIA.

Let's see. [*Putting her hand on his forehead.*] Poor dear ! your head is hot—absolutely feverish !

ERNEST, *unwarily*.

Yes—that's it.

VIRGINIA, *seizing her opportunity*.

Yes, dear. [*Soothingly*] Let me keep my hand here—it will cool your forehead.

ERNEST, *equal to the situation*.

No, my dear. [*Removing the cooler.*] It wouldn't be proper.

VIRGINIA, *to herself, as she retires*.

It won't do. I must try something stronger. For a *débutant*, he takes care of himself pretty well. [*Aloud*] Ernest, do you know of what I am thinking ?

ERNEST.

Of nothing, probably.

VIRGINIA, *impulsively*.

The impertinent fellow ! [*Aside, recollecting herself*] But no. It's his part. That's the way we women do. [*She returns to the attack.*] No,

Ernest, I was thinking of your youth—of the happy days when we were children. Have you forgotten them? [*Pensively*] We were always together then. We had no other friends. We lived a life apart from other children. You were my Paul, and I was your Virginia.

ERNEST, *heartlessly*.

Oh, yes, I remember. A romance in duodecimo—idyls—pastorals—the regular business. But you get over that sort of thing as you grow older, you know. There isn't much wear to it.

VIRGINIA, *aside*.

He is getting positively outrageous now. [*Aloud, with a sudden change in tone*] Stay, Ernest, it is better that we should stop here. Perhaps—perhaps—we have gone too far already. I have been too . . . . reckless in lending myself to this comedy. We must not play with love like this! [*She seats herself, and rests her head on her hand.*]

ERNEST.

Virginia! [*Aside*] What's all this?

VIRGINIA, *nervously*.

It is not impossible that—without knowing it —that my heart should cease to be insensible— that my laughter of this morning should change to tears before the evening. Even now, it seems to me, I tremble at the thought of the strange game we are playing. What if, in this jest, I should betray myself? [*Growing more and more excited.*] What if — I learned to *love* you? [*Aside*] We'll see, this time!

ERNEST, *on his feet.*

What! Is it true? You might—you might —love me? Yes, yes, for *I* love you! Cousin— Virginia—my own! Don't check this impulse of your heart—it speaks the truth. Why should you not give me your heart, as you have taught me to give you—

VIRGINIA, *with a peal of laughter.*

One dollar!

ERNEST, *taken aback.*

One dollar!

VIRGINIA.

Yes—a counter—a forfeit. Caught this time.

ERNEST, *solemnly reseating himself.*

'Twasn't fair.

VIRGINIA.

Why not?

ERNEST.

Because I wasn't caught.

VIRGINIA.

You weren't . . . .

ERNEST.

I wasn't caught.   No.

VIRGINIA.

Then why did you respond in that way ?

ERNEST.

Well, my dear, the circumstances—after what you have said, you know—politeness required—I could do no less.

VIRGINIA.

Do you mean to say that I didn't deceive you ?

ERNEST.

Not in the least.

VIRGINIA, *warmly*.

You didn't believe, when I spoke to you just now, that I was beginning to feel for you a—a tender sentiment ?

ERNEST, *with shameless mendacity*.

I did not believe it.

VIRGINIA, *growing excited*.

Explain yourself, sir !   You were not serious, then, when you answered me ?

ERNEST.

I was jesting—as you were.

VIRGINIA, *exploding.*

And you dared! You had the audacity! Ah, now I believe you have been jesting from the first—this love you have always expressed—it was a jest, too!

ERNEST, *languidly.*

You don't think *that.*

VIRGINIA.

I do! Ah! it is a good lesson to me. That is the way we women are deceived. What fools we are! It was just the same air, the same accent —the same words, the same look of adoration. 'Twas no better done when you meant it—but you never meant it. If you can imitate love so well, you can never have felt it. I have unmasked you. We will settle this matter. [*Marching from right to left, up and down the room.*] We'll see—we'll see! What! You don't answer me? No—you *can't!* Be silent—it is the best thing you can do! Oh, if I spoke my mind—you—you—impostor! I can not restrain myself! I'm going—and I'll never—never—see you again!

And she departs, L. U. E., like a small feminine hurricane. Yet the bang of the door seems to cover something like a sob. The wretched impostor sits still, as a man conscious of his own iniquity. But, as he meditates, a puzzled look begins to overspread his features. With less depression in his tone than becomes the situation, he murmurs to himself:

Well, I swear ! Well, I swear ! Well, I
swear ! I'll swear she was going to cry !

The striking of a clock and the simultaneous opening of
the door disturb his profane reverie. VIRGINIA appears on the
threshold. She may have been " going to cry," but she certainly
shows no signs of having yielded to the impulse. She is bright,
laughing, and triumphant.

VIRGINIA.

Ernest, dinner ! The game is over ! You remember the agreement. I exact strict adherence
to the terms therein expressed. From this time
until my departure, you are not to whisper one
word of love to me.

ERNEST.

Unless you ask me to.

VIRGINIA, *laughing.*

Unless I ask you to—that was agreed.

ERNEST, *calmly.*

And you will also be so kind as to remember
that I still retain nine counters, and that each of
them represents a—kiss.

VIRGINIA, *with icy resignation.*

I suppose I must submit.

ERNEST.

No.

VIRGINIA.

What ?

ERNEST.

No.   No doubt it would be very delightful to press my lips to your cheek, if but one look invited me.   But *thus*—No ! your calmness speaks without disguise.   The charm is destroyed.   You know, yourself, the contact of lips is nothing—it is the emotion, the soul of the kiss, that I seek.

VIRGINIA.

Excuse me, sir.   You may be doing violence to your feelings in kissing me ; but I insist—I have my reasons.   At this price I shall be finally freed from your importunities ; you shall fulfill your part of the bargain.   Come, sir, treaties are made for the benefit of the victor.   If you are generous—you will kiss me.

ERNEST, *graver.*

Very well—I will obey, since honor compels me.   [*Going toward her as she stands at center.*] You are blushing.

VIRGINIA.

No, I'm not.

ERNEST.

Yes, you are, I say.

VIRGINIA, *impatiently.*

No, sir !   No.   I'm ready.

The victim turns her cheek to the recalcitrant conqueror, who exacts his tribute with hesitating reluctance. VIRGINIA shivers nervously, and ERNEST frowns darkly, like a captive pirate on the point of execution.

ERNEST.

This is—cruel.   But it must be done, and one gets accustomed to everything.   Eight more.

VIRGINIA.

No, I beg of you !

ERNEST.

Eight kisses, if you please.

VIRGINIA.

But just now you didn't care about them at all.

ERNEST.

But just now you cared about them a good deal.

VIRGINIA.

But, then—since—O Ernest—please don't insist.

ERNEST.

Why not ?   Is it that—you love me ?

VIRGINIA.

No—not a bit.   What is troubling me is— are—those eight counters.

ERNEST.

You don't like the gross amount of kissing they represent ?

VIRGINIA.

No.

ERNEST.

Well. There's a way to stop all that kind of thing.

VIRGINIA.

What is it ?

ERNEST.

Marry ! 'Twon't trouble you any more after that.

VIRGINIA, *looking down.*

Isn't there any other way ?

ERNEST.

Not that I know of.

VIRGINIA.

Oh, dear !

A pause.

ERNEST.

Come, Virginia, decide.

VIRGINIA.

Decide—what ?

ERNEST.

Whether you'll marry me or not.

VIRGINIA.

Who was talking about marrying ?

ERNEST, *with business-like precision.*

I was ; and you were, too.

VIRGINIA.

Well, don't talk any more—at least not to-day —to-morrow.

ERNEST.

And what do you wish me to do to-morrow ?

VIRGINIA.

Oh, you may—you may ask any questions you want to.   And [*with a smile*] I *may* answer them.

ERNEST.

I haven't any questions to ask.

VIRGINIA.

You haven't ?

ERNEST.

No.   Virginia, we set out to play "Courtship with Variations," and play it we shall.   It may be a shade frivolous and foolish, our comedy ; but it is I who have the dangerous rôle—that of the *ingénue.*   You are the lover—I am the true and tender woman.   Make your proposal.

VIRGINIA, *with startling suddenness.*

I will! [*Gravely*] Sir! Recognizing in you the possessor of many excellent qualities; regarding you as a young man of amiability, good moral character, and—

ERNEST.

And?

VIRGINIA.

Vast pertinacity, together with *some* charms of person—regarding you thus, I say, a young friend of mine desires that I should speak in her name. She finds existence a sad feast, when unshared with any other loving heart. She feels that, to be truly comfortable, affection must sit opposite one at table and carve the roast beef. Will you undertake the discharge of these functions? Come, blush, for form's sake, and say—

ERNEST, *with ingenuous confusion.*

Yes!

They slowly sidle toward one another, and at the point of meeting, with the suddenness of an electric shock, they resume their personal identities, which they appear about to fuse in a cousinly embrace.

ERNEST, *suddenly recollecting himself.*

But stop—what am I doing? It was agreed that I was not to breathe another word of love to you.

VIRGINIA.

Unless—I asked you to.

ERNEST.

Well, do you ?

VIRGINIA, *shyly.*

Do you think it would be very much out of
place in

COURTSHIP WITH VARIATIONS ?

ERNEST does not seem to think it would.

QUICK CURTAIN.

A TEACHER TAUGHT.

COMEDY IN ONE ACT.

By A. H. OAKES.

CHARACTERS.

Frederick Belfort, Ph. D., *Professor of Inorganic Chemistry at the Metropolitan University, 35 years old.*

Kate Winstanley, *his ward and pupil, 18 years old.*

.

[The French original of this play is " *Le Roman d'une Pupille*," written by M. Paul Ferrier.]

A TEACHER TAUGHT.

SCENE : Professor Belfort's study—a plainly furnished room. Writing-table, covered with
papers, L. C. Door R. U. E. Bookcase Left
side of room [not necessarily practicable].
Scientific apparatus, etc., disposed about
room. General aspect gloomy and dull.

THE PROFESSOR, *alone.*

What's that I hear ?
   [*Going to door L. U. E. and speaking off.*
    Lunch ? For the sake of—pity !
Here's my report not yet half written, Kitty.
Science and I are conquering vulgar doubt,
And Luncheon comes to put us both clean out.
Postpone it, Kitty. [*Kate laughs, off stage.*
    Ah ! that silvery laugh !
Too much for science and for me, by half.
There, dear, I promise, next time, on my word,
To be as punctual as the early bird.
My life shall be the forfeit. Yes, I own it,

I *am* "just horrid."   Well, you *will* postpone it?
A half an hour ?

I knew she would, God bless her !
Too gentle to the stupid old Professor.

[*He sits at table R.*
Sweet little Kate !   I'm doing wrong, in truth,
To let her waste the blossom of her youth
In this dull house, slaving for dull old me.
And yet I can't—
[*With sudden resolution*]

Hang it, I must !

[*Turns to his writing*]   Let's see !
"This gas is strictly not a gas, but rather—"
Look here, Professor, you're a precious father.
These serious duties you've assumed, are you
Quite sure you've conscientiously gone through ?
The child of thirteen summers is to-day
A woman—a "young lady."   Come, we'll say
You've taught her Latin, Greek, and Mathematics,
Algebra, Botany, and Hydrostatics,
History, Geography, and Physics—verily,
You've done this thoroughly—and unnecessarily.
O wise preceptor ! with pedantic goad
Urging the tender mind to bear this load.
Putting a sweet child's youth upon the shelf
To make her like your sciolistic self.
At cost of happiness growing over-wise—
She can't be happy thus.   .

She has blue eyes
And golden hair, and cheeks of rose and white,

And I have set her Latin themes to write !
She's sweet eighteen ; she's pretty, and she's
    gay.
My Kitty's probably inclined to play.
She'll learn to love balls, dancing, admiration ;
And then, of course, come young men, and flirta-
    tion.
They'll find her pretty.　That I must expect, too.
Further, they'll say so.
               This I may object to.
Well, well, a selfish gardener, my flower,
My one, I've hidden in a gloomy bower—
Robbed it of freedom, as of light and air !
Knowing it dear, forgot that it was fair.
Yes, she must wed.　And may the happy wife
Forget the girl's sad solitary life.
And may she find some not impossible he,
Young, gay—the very opposite of me.
And may the lucky devil love my Kate
More wisely, and as well as I—
        [*Looking at clock*]　So late !
Oh ! my report !　Let's see, again no use ?
Science and gas may both go to the—deuce.

Enter KATE *L. U. E.*

           KATE.
May I come in ?
        THE PROFESSOR.
      Of course !

KATE.

Here is a letter
Marked "most important"—but perhaps I'd
    better
Let the epistle with my luncheon wait
Till the report—

THE PROFESSOR.

Unscientific Kate !
Give me the note, drop that irreverent air,
And [*reads*]—hm-hm-hm ! This, dear, is your
    affair.

KATE.

Mine ? Who's the writer ?

THE PROFESSOR.

Buckingham de Brown,
My pupil, he who was to settle down
And study chemistry—which branch has missed
A very dandified young scientist,
Whose careless laugh bids serious thought avaunt—
He's just the very husband that you want.

KATE.

The husband !

THE PROFESSOR.

Yes, the very husband ! .Pray
Listen to me, my dear. This very day
I had recalled a duty long neglected ;
That letter is no more than I'd expected.

KATE.

But, if you please, what is all this to me ?

THE PROFESSOR.

That's true, I didn't mention.   Well, you see,
Just listen then to Buckingham : " My dear,
My most respected master "—So far, clear ?

KATE.

Quite.

THE PROFESSOR.

Well, you see, I couldn't but remember
That you were May, if I was—ah—September.
Not with my logical train of thought to bore
     you—
I felt that I must seek a husband for you.
Of course, you notice the necessity ?

KATE, *crossing to L.*

You're in a hurry to get rid of me ?
So, sir, to settle my hymeneal fate,
Till long past noon you've let my luncheon wait ?

THE PROFESSOR.

Kitty !

KATE, *crossing R.*

I thought you deep in your report—
Had I suspected anything of this sort—

THE PROFESSOR.

Indeed, I—

KATE.

No excuse ! it's rankest treason
Against my welfare, without rhyme or reason.
Why spend the time Science might better fill
In marrying me off against my will ?

THE PROFESSOR.

Aha ! I see.   The persecuted ward—
The cruel guardian—the unwelcome lord.
What, would the fairest maiden ever seen
Braid the gray tresses of St. Katharine ?

KATE.

I didn't say that.

THE PROFESSOR.

Then the bridegroom meant
Is hateful ?

KATE.

Not quite that—indifferent.

THE PROFESSOR.

The ground for your objection I can't see
Quite clear.

KATE.

You wish to marry him to me ?

THE PROFESSOR.

He asks it.

KATE.

Well, it shall be as you say:
You are my guardian—I can but obey.

THE PROFESSOR.

My dear, your choice shall be your own, of
    course.
I don't habitually use brute force.
But see—I am your guardian and your tutor :
From these two standpoints do I view your
    suitor.
I judge him by known quantities, and find
The youth quite tolerable—never mind !
I'm thirty-five, old, crabbed, and pedantic;
You are eighteen, and possibly romantic.
You've formed your own ideal of a lover—
You want your romance — Buckingham goes
    over.
So much for him.

KATE.

        I think you take a pleasure
In planning to dismiss me, sir !

THE PROFESSOR.

                My treasure !
Dismiss you ! That is, to dismiss the light,
The life of my poor house—to exile outright
The gracious spirit, the delightful fay,
Whose magic wiles the weary hours away.
Only at duty's bidding am I fain
To break my willing little captive's chain.
I shall be lonely when you leave me—

KATE.

                                Who
Has spoken of leaving you ?

THE PROFESSOR.

                    Not I, nor you,
But common sense and reason.   Fate lays out
The path of every mortal.   You forget
How long we've walked together, you and I.
It's more than time we separated.

KATE.

                        Why ?

THE PROFESSOR.

"Why ?"   Do you ask ?   My task is ended now.
My friend, your dying father, made me vow
That I would take his place—

KATE.

                    And well, dear friend,
You have kept your vow.   Heaven took *him*, but
        to lend
A dearer father to the lonely child,
Who wept, abandoned; learned to love, and
        smiled.
I have never known a parent, saving you,
Nor ever felt the loss, nor ever knew
Where else to bring the love and gratitude
I owe to you, so tender and so good.
In all my childish joys and sorrows—

THE PROFESSOR.

Crying!
Kitty, my dear! Please don't! I'm only trying
To make things pleasant.

KATE, *still sobbing*.

Oh, indeed, quite charming!

THE PROFESSOR.

I can't see that the prospect's so alarming.
You'll have a quiet, obedient little spouse,
And stay and share the old Professor's house,
And he sha'n't part us.

KATE.

But I do not see
Why there is any need of marrying me.

THE PROFESSOR.

My duty. I have told you once, my dear—
Your happiness.

KATE.

My happiness is here.

THE PROFESSOR.

To that kind compliment I'm quite alive.
But ah! I know I'm old—

KATE, *laughing*.

Yes! Thirty—

THE PROFESSOR.

Five !

Full five-and-thirty.

KATE.

Five-and-thirty you'd
Think marked the confines of decrepitude.
My eyes may play me false, but yet among
The younger men you seem to me as young.
And you yourself know, I could never say
"Papa" to you.

THE PROFESSOR.

O flatterer, away !

KATE.

No flattery !   Get some gray hairs before
I can believe you old.

THE PROFESSOR.

You ask no more ?
A gray peruke without delay I'll don—
One with a bald spot.

KATE.

Well, that's getting on.

THE PROFESSOR.

And then we'll speak of marrying you ?

KATE.

Oh, come !
Marriage, like charity, should begin at home.

You who on marrying all the world are bent,
Why don't *you* marry?

THE PROFESSOR.
1? That's different.

KATE.
"Do unto others as you'd have them do
To you." Please say, is the reverse not true?

THE PROFESSOR.
A right sound doctrine! But, all jest aside,
I've never married; but—because—she died.

KATE.
Oh, pardon me!

THE PROFESSOR.
Well, from that day I vowed
My life to study; kinder fate allowed
That you should fill the heart that bled for her:
And I, by memory left a widower,
And by my love for you, a father, thought
My broken life was rounded—

KATE.
Which you ought
Not! Most decidedly. What if happiness
Once more this "broken" life of yours should
bless,
Can you think truly the beloved shade
You mourn would envy you?

THE PROFESSOR.
                    But what fair maid
Would smile upon me now?

KATE.
                    I know one or two
That I could mention.

THE PROFESSOR.
                    You have known me blue,
Humdrum and stupid, misanthropic, slow;
Pedant and bookworm, rusty as a crow;
Bent o'er my books—I've almost got a hunch—
And never ready at the hour of lunch.

KATE.
I have known you good, and modest, too, about it;
Wise without pedantry, though you seem to
        doubt it;
Kind, and still kinder than the world has known;
A kindness shown to, guessed by, me alone.
And she would have just reason to rejoice
On whom might fall the honor of your choice.

THE PROFESSOR.
A list of virtues which would scarcely steal
The heart of a young lady—

KATE.
                    I appeal
From that unrighteous verdict. Do you hold
All girls so frivolous?

THE PROFESSOR.

No, not when they're old.

KATE.

Indeed ! Your mood's sarcastic, sir, to-day.
Believe me, there are some quite different !

THE PROFESSOR.

Nay !

Deceiver worst of all, can even your flattery
Call me respectable in my—my—cravattery ?
    [*touching his necktie.*]
Is this old coat with foxy velvet collar
The fashion ? Wouldn't, say, a half a dollar
Be well laid out in treating to new soles
These shoes ? My shirts would be but button-
        holes
Were't not for you.   And, worst of all my faults,
Have I the faintest notion of a waltz ?
Of talent, charm, or grace, have I one jot ?
Would *you* take such a husband ?

KATE.

Well, why not ?

THE PROFESSOR.

Dear child ! You're very young and innocent,
And I—blind bookworm o'er my folios bent—
Have never told you life may yet disclose
Another love than child to father owes ;

And that some day—but I have been too fast :
I thought you a woman—you're a child—

KATE.

At last !

I thought 'twould come.   *In toto* I deny
The soft impeachment.—Child, indeed !   Not I.
I am a woman !   And my woman's heart
Has known that love already—felt its smart.
I have had my romance—not a happy one.
The sunflower of my life has found its sun.

THE PROFESSOR.

What — no — it can't be !   Ah, I might have
        known !
Already—loving—secret and alone.
And I guessed nothing.   Yes, I see it now—
Your late refusal.   And I noticed how
You started when I spoke.   What could say more
Clear that the little heart had throbbed before ?
Who is your hero, then ?—Who is it ?   Say !
Handsome and young ?   Brilliant. and polished—
        gay ?
And does he know that he has won possession
Of that sweet heart ?   Come, let's have full con-
        fession !

KATE.

Handsome ?—Perhaps !   I know that he is good.
Young ?—Well, I think he could be, if he would.
Less brilliant than profound ; less gay than true.

As far as I'm concerned, he—oh, he'll do !
I have known him at your house. I have loved
    him—well—
Always ! But yet I've never dared to tell.
And now I'm very much afraid I sha'n't
Unless he—helps me—when he sees—I can't !
I think he'll have to guess—I'd rather not.
I'm going now—to keep that luncheon hot !
        [*Exit precipitately L. U. E.*

THE PROFESSOR, *alone.*

Kate ! I—confound it—I am dreaming—no !
Yes ! What's the lucky devil's name ?—don't go !
His name ! By Jove ! I must have fallen asleep,
And dreamed. It strikes me I have dreamed a—
    heap.
No, I'm awake. My wits have ta'en an airing.
Asleep or crazy ? Neither ! I am staring,
Stark wide awake. Fates adverse and propitious !
What hear I ? Things impossibly delicious.
Yet real—unpermissible and real.
That is important. I am her ideal.
Is it—any other fellow, if not me ?
No ! Can't mistake it—it's too plain to see
She loves me. I am sure of it—I know it.
That's what she meant. Didn't her features
    show it ?
And I ? My heart I thought dead all the while
Is beating in a rather lively style.
My blood's on fire ! I feel just like a—star.

Kate ! I'm in love, dear—more so than you are.
But no. The devil ! This will never do.
I'm but a father to her. 'Tisn't true—
Poor little thing, so good, so innocent—
For love she takes a child's fond sentiment.
'Tis madness—sweet to me, but madness still.
And I must cure it, cost me what it will.

Enter KATE, *L. U. E., with the luncheon.*

KATE.

The luncheon, sir.

THE PROFESSOR, *huskily.*
My daughter !

KATE, *aside.*
Daughter ! gracious !
His way of guessing things is—is vexatious !

THE PROFESSOR.
Come here, my child.

KATE.
I come.

THE PROFESSOR.
I've understood.

KATE, *aside.*
Upon my word, I rather thought he would.

THE PROFESSOR.

I know your hero.

KATE, *aside.*

This is perspicacity
Indeed !

THE PROFESSOR.

Although it took some slight audacity
To recognize the flattering portrait.   Yet,
My Kate, think calmly if your heart is set
Upon a love that may be, at the most,
A warmer gratitude.   I can but boast
Poor paltry claims, that your too kindly eyes
Exaggerate, to this too generous prize.
You are young, and louder than cool reason's voice
Impulse may speak, and guide a childish choice.
When the young heart is filled with love's soft
        light,
All things it looks on catch the radiance bright.
You scarcely realize, I'm sore afraid,
The shade you take for love—and such a shade !
But he you think you love knows all too well
Your error : knows his duty is to tell
What sacrifice, unconscious though it be,
This dream entails.   A cruel guardian he
Who thus would cheat his child.   My little Kate !
Your debt of gratitude, with usurer's rate
Of interest, you paid me long ago.
If debt there be, 'tis what to you I owe.

Pride of my home, joy of my heart—oh say,
Is it a debt that I shall ever pay ?

KATE.

Then, my Professor, none may give *you* love,
Whose eloquence a heart of stone would move,
Whose burning words would render, I believe,
A Romeo jealous ?   You can not conceive
A woman's heart must yield itself to one
Who sings of love—as—well, as you have done ?

THE PROFESSOR.

But, Kate !

KATE.

You're better pleased the account to cast
So that the balance to my side is passed—
To search arithmetic and logic through
To prove by *A* plus *B* I don't love you.

THE PROFESSOR.

I cry you mercy !

KATE.

To your will I bow.
You were my guardian ever, and are now.
You're wisdom's self. My eighteen years are wrong:
Guide then my bark, since your own hand's so
    strong.
Before your great experience I incline.
To prove how I mistrust this will of mine—
Write to De Brown, then, that at your command
I accept his—love—his fortune, and his hand.

THE PROFESSOR.

Do you accept ?

KATE.

His hand, his fortune—

THE PROFESSOR.

You're
Not jesting ? *He* your husband ! Are you sure ?

KATE.

Why not ? He's young, destined to cut a dash,
Handsome—and such a wee—wee—wee mustache !

THE PROFESSOR.

You are laughing.

KATE.

No. He is a good *parti;*
A well-assorted couple we shall be.
He's of good family, and, it's only fair
To mention also, he's a millionaire.

THE PROFESSOR.

I know you better than to think you speak
Your mind in this. Your judgment's not so
    weak
As that, my Kate. Your heart is not so cold.
You're not a girl to love a sack of gold.
Say what you may, I don't believe you care
For Brown, were he ten times a millionaire.
You can not like him, and, to tell the truth,

10

I don't, myself, greatly admire the youth.
A boy, as boys go, good enough, agreed—
But not the one to marry *you*.

KATE.

Indeed !

THE PROFESSOR.

A shallow dandy—a mere mutton-head,
Who puts on mighty airs ; snobbish, half-bred ;
Ignorant, careless, loose, unscientific ;
Of good works barren and of debts prolific.
Laziest of men, unwilling or unable
To read a book.   At home in club or stable,
But nowhere else—a man who will, of course,
Divide his love between you and—his horse.

KATE, *aside.*

I thought so.

THE PROFESSOR.

He's unworthy such a treasure.
Look elsewhere for a husband.

KATE.

At your pleasure.
Just as you say.   But I supposed you knew
I was but doing as you told me to.

THE PROFESSOR.

Well—but—I thought—

KATE.

You see, one may mistake
At any age.   But what choice *shall* I make ?
Young Buckingham de Brown is, we will say,
A type of all the young men of the day.
If this be so, and if we won't have him,
The chances of the rest grow rather slim.
In very truth, as far as I can see,
I'll never get a husband—

THE PROFESSOR.

Kate, take *me!*

KATE.

You ?

THE PROFESSOR.

Yes, my love, you wanted to, just now.

KATE.

Oh, but, since then, you know, you've shown me
      how
I erred in such a choice.   And to the letter
I'll follow your advice.

THE PROFESSOR.

For want of better !

KATE.

Well, it might do, if you were not so old.

THE PROFESSOR.

So old ?

KATE.

Yes, thirty-five.

THE PROFESSOR.

I never told
Any one that ! My birthday is next week.
I'm thirty-four at present.

KATE.

So to speak,
That's middle-aged.

THE PROFESSOR.

I haven't one gray hair—
In my whole head.

KATE.

Well, they'll soon be there.

THE PROFESSOR.

No, I'll be bald first.

KATE.

But you never go
Into society.

THE PROFESSOR.

But I will, you know.

KATE.

Your dress adds to your years full eight or nine.

THE PROFESSOR.

Buckingham de Brown's own tailor shall be mine.

KATE.

Algebra 'll be my rival, I foresee.

THE PROFESSOR.

Only to prove my love by A plus B.

KATE.

You'll not be ready when the lunch-bell rings.

THE PROFESSOR.

'Twill be your task to teach me all those things.

KATE.

But then, my guardian, is.it your advice
That I should make this awful sacrifice ?

THE PROFESSOR.

You saucy jade !

KATE.

   And only as a daughter
Can a girl love the patriarch who's taught her
To say "papa !"

THE PROFESSOR.

   No—that I did not—never !
O Kate ! you're laughing. Oh, you saucy, clever,

Malicious—angel!   Jove enthroned above!
Mars!   Gods eleven, I have won her love!
Her love!   Yes, I was idiotic, blind,
Not to have guessed it.   Kitty, never mind!
We'll make up for lost time now — wait and
    see—
I love you, dear, more even than you love me.

CURTAIN.

HEREDITY.

A PHYSIOLOGICAL AND PSYCHOLOGICAL ABSURDITY IN ONE ACT.

By ARTHUR PENN.

CHARACTERS.

Mr. Smith, *a burgomaster.*

Mr. Smith, *a drum major.*

Mr. Smith, *a swell.*

Mr. Smith, *a sporting gentleman.*

Mr. von Bruckencruckenthal, *a gentleman suffering from compatibility of temper.*

Mrs. von Bruckencruckenthal, *a lady suffering from the same cause.*

Miss Bella Smith, *a young lady of great personal attractions, who falls heir finally—but perhaps it is as well not to anticipate.*

[The French original of this play is "*La Postérité d'un Bourgmestre*," written by M. Mario Uchard.]

HEREDITY.*

SCENE : A public square in Hackendrackenstackenfelstein, a small German village near the
Rhine.   Burgomaster's house L., with practi-
cable window over the door.   Chair before the
door.   The Dew Drop Inn R., with a swing-
ing sign.   Chair and table before its door.

*Burgomaster discovered C. between Mr. and
Mrs. von Bruckencruckenthal.   Other villagers R. and L.*

OPENING CHORUS.

Air : "Upidee " or " The Cork Leg."

They say it is the proper thing
That we an opening chorus sing;
And so we stand here in a ring
To raise our voice from wing to wing.

Although we do not think it nice,
A single verse will not suffice;
More are included in the price,
And so we have to bore you twice.

[Exeunt villagers R. and L.

* See Prefatory Note, p. 13, for remarks about the performance of this play.

BURGOMASTER.

Now, Mr. and Mrs. von Bruckcruckenthal, I give you five minutes, not a second more. Before being Burgomaster, I was Colonel in the First Hackendrackenstackenfelstein Mounted Fire Extinguishers. To-day is the anniversary of the capture of Holzenstolzenburg. As an old soldier, I take part in the ceremony. I had already donned my Colonel's costume when you knocked, and concealed the warrior under the robe of the magistrate. The sun will shortly appear. I give you five minutes. Speak !

VON B.

Well—you see—your honor.

BURGOMASTER, *interrupting.*

Tell me quickly, what do you desire, Mr. von Truck ?

VON B., *correcting.*

Von Bruckencruckenthal, your honor. I want to be divorced.

BURGOMASTER.

And you, Mrs. von Truck ?

VON B., *correcting.*

Von Bruckencruckenthal.

MRS. VON B.

So do I, your honor. I could not think of opposing my husband.

BURGOMASTER.

What are your reasons ? Is your wife disagreeable ?

VON B.

On the contrary.

BURGOMASTER.

Extravagant ?

MRS. VON B.

He carries the purse, your honor.

BURGOMASTER.

Does she flirt ?

VON B.

Never, your honor.

BURGOMASTER.

Does she beat you ?

MRS. VON B.

Oh, no ! I love him too much for that.

BURGOMASTER.

Well, then, if it is not impertinent, I should like to know why you want a divorce.

VON B.

For compatibility of temper.

BURGOMASTER.

Very well, for incompatibility of temper.

Von B.

No, your honor, I said compatibility of temper.

Burgomaster.

I would comprehend.   I do not comprehend.

Von B.

I will explain, your honor.   When I want a thing, my wife desires exactly the same thing. When I want to go to the right, she says go to the right.   The dishes I like she adores.   I say scissors, she says scissors.   The infernal similarity in our tastes, our ideas, in fact, in everything, makes my life wretchedly one-sided.   Existence is insupportable.   I need variety, excitement, and not this disgusting monotony.. That's why I want a divorce.

Burgomaster.

What say you, Mrs. von Truck?

Von B., *correcting.*

Von Bruckencruckenthal.

Mrs. von B.

Nothing, your honor.   My husband must be right, since he is my husband.

Von B.

Just hear that, your honor.

BURGOMASTER.

Enough ! the five minutes have elapsed. Mrs. von Brokencrockery, come here. [*Whispers to Mrs. van B.*]

VON B., *aside.*

What is he saying to her ? Oh ! if I don't get a divorce, this devastating monotony will kill me.

BURGOMASTER, *to Mrs. von B.*

To be taken every morning and evening, before meals. [*To von B.*] Mr. von Brokencrockery, come and see me in a week. Good day. The Burgomaster vanishes. [*Exit L.*

VON B.

What did he whisper you ?

MRS. VON B.

He told me of a remedy to correct myself.

VON B.

You don't say so ! What remedy ?

MRS. VON B., *boxing his ears.*

That !

VON B.

What ?

MRS. VON B.

Every morning and evening, before meals.

Von B.

We'll see about that.

Mrs. von B.

Forward—march—look sharp!

Von B.

Here is a remedy of the patent-medicine kind.

Mrs. von B.

But it will succeed.   [*Exeunt R.*

BURGOMASTER *enters L. from house in fantastic costume of Mounted Fire Extinguishers, without his boots. He strikes a solemn attitude before his door, and then sneezes.*

BURGOMASTER.

Atchi! The dream was strange. All night I saw my son, my long-lost son. If I could only recover him! Perhaps the dream was a heavenly warning. I have long hoped that some lucky accident would bring us face to face, and that a father's heart— [*Comes down C.*] It was in 1832. He was six years old. We bivouacked on the banks of the Kalbsbratenthaler. Suddenly we were attacked by guerrillas—no, gorillas—no, guerrillas. We seize our arms—I tell my son to await my return near a tree—I mount my steed— we fly to victory—the enemy fly from us—and I fly to the arms of Murphy—no, Morphy—I mean

Morpheus. The next day I return for my son. I found the tree. I had blazed it with my sabre; but my son was—gone. [*Chord.*] I interrogate the police—the detectives—but, of course, they knew nothing. Since then, no news. I have become Burgomaster. Once a year I rebecome Colonel. [*Poetically*] Here comes the dawn. Aurora, smiling child of Phœbus. Atchi! [*Sneezes —then goes up and sits before door, taking out paper from pocket.*] Let's see the news. "The Daily Comet." I like "The Daily Comet"—it always has such good tales. "Telegraphic News. By Cable. Associated Press Dispatches. Holzenstolzenfels: The event of the day is the *début* at the Royal Senegambian Circus of the riding manmonkey, the Cynocephalus." [*Spoken*] Cynocephalus—pretty name—'tis a German name. [*Reads*] "This prodigy of strength—this hairy *artiste*—" [*Spoken*] *Artiste.* Ah! he's an Italian. [*Reads*] "This hairy *artiste* performs the most difficult feats with a facility extremely surprising. His best act is the Flying Leap of the Bounding Antelope of the Choctaw Desert." [*Rises*] Ah! the father of such a son may well be proud. My Edward would perhaps have resembled him. My Edward! Oh, that dream! If I should only recover him, I would make him my friend, my companion, my boot-black. Ah! away with weakness. I am a burgomaster—that is some consolation. Atchi! [*Sneezes.*]

SMITH, *a swell, enters L., with sack on back, cane, eyeglass, etc.   Very strong lisp throughout. Reads sign of inn.*

SWELL.

By Jove! this is it.   The Dew Drop Inn. [*To Burgomaster*] I say, my friend, does the Flying Velocipede pass here for Holzenstolzenfels?

BURGOMASTER, *majestically.*

In the first place, I am not your friend.   In the second place, you will immediately show me your passport.

SWELL, *taking off sack.*

By Jove! ye know, my passport is in my sack, my good man.

BURGOMASTER, *indignantly.*

I am not your good man.   Your passport!

SWELL.

Give a fellow time, you know.   You'll see, my name is Smith.

BURGOMASTER, *aside, excitedly.*

Heavens!   That eye! that mouth! those nose!   If it were he!   [*Aloud*] Your name is Smith?

SWELL.

Yes, Colonel.

BURGOMASTER.

Call me Burgomaster.

SWELL, *giving passport.*

There, enraged wretch !

BURGOMASTER, *taking it tenderly.*

Call me friend. [*Reads, aside.*] Heavens !
he told the truth. [*Aloud*] Young man, your
hand. I am also a Smith.

SWELL.

You are no phenomenon, dilapidated individual. I know many more Smiths, without
counting my father.

BURGOMASTER, *wildly.*

You have a father ?

SWELL.

By Jove ! ye know. Do I look as if I grew on
a rose-tree, agèd innocent ? [*Sneezes.*] Atchi !
There, I am catching cold.

BURGOMASTER, *with joy, struck by an idea, aside.*

He has a cold. I have a cold. Perhaps it is
hereditary. [*Aloud*] Young man, you resemble
a son I lost. [*Embraces him.*]

SWELL, *struggling.*

By Jove ! ye know ; he is mad. Wrathy curiosity, restrain your emotion.

11

BURGOMASTER, *putting hand to Swell's heart.*
You feel nothing there ?

SWELL, *roughly.*
I feel a No. 11 hand. [*Repulses Burgomaster, and sits at table R., eating bread and cherries from sack.*]

BURGOMASTER, *L.*
How he resembles me ! This is mysterious —very mysterious ! I must dissemble. [*Retires up L.*]

BELLA *enters R. with a small package in her hand.*

Ah ! Oh, dear ! Isn't it hot ! [*Puts package on table; sees Swell.*] Ah ! a young man. Good day, sir. [*Courtesies.*]

SWELL, *at table R.*
By Jove ! ye know. What a pretty girl !

BURGOMASTER, *coming down R.*
Female peasantess, your passport !

BELLA.
Oh, dear ! a soldier. Good day, sir. [*Courtesies.*]

BURGOMASTER, *severely.*
Your passport !

BELLA, *giving it.*
There, sir.

BURGOMASTER, *taking it.*

Your name!

BELLA.

Bella Smith, sir.

BURGOMASTER, *aside, excitedly.*

Smith! [*Reads.*] Heavens! 'tis true. That eye! that mouth! those nose! If it were he! [*To Bella*] You are a girl?

BELLA, *laughing.*

If you please, your honor, don't be stupid!

BURGOMASTER, *dignified.*

Female peasantess, your language is incendiary! Remember that I represent the law, and to say I am stupid—

BELLA.

Oh, dear! I beg your pardon, sir; it was a slip of the tongue. [*Innocently*] I know I should not always say what I think.

BURGOMASTER, *majestically.*

'Tis well! [*Slowly exit L.*

BELLA, *looking at him, laughs.*

Oh, dear! ins't he funny? Some men are so ugly.

SWELL.

Thank you for them.

BELLA, *quickly*.

Oh! I don't say that for you; you are quite good-looking.

SWELL.

Thank you for myself.

BELLA, *confused*.

Oh, dear! that was another slip.

SWELL.

By Jove! ye know, I don't complain. I would say as much to you.

BELLA, *sitting at table R.*

Oh, bah! We don't know each other.

SWELL.

By Jove! ye know, we must. Which way do you go?

BELLA.

That doesn't interest you; you won't come.

SWELL.

By Jove! ye know, you don't know me. I've followed girls far plainer than you.

BELLA, *conceitedly*.

I should say so.

SWELL.

Coquette!

BELLA, *confusedly.*

Oh, dear ! that was a slip.

SWELL, *offering fruit.*

Have some cherries ?

BELLA, *taking fruit.*

Yes, a few—a very few. Oh, ain't they awful nice !

SWELL.

You love fruit, like all Eve's daughters.

BELLA, *eating.*

Eve's daughters ? Don't know them. They don't live in this part of the country.

SWELL.

So you won't tell me which way you go ?

BELLA, *rising.*

Oh, dear ! You are too inquisitive. I don't answer such questions [*very fast*], although Mrs. Jackman does say I'm a chatterbox. It is not that Mrs. Jackman is a bad sort of woman. Oh, dear, no ! but you see she is selling her house.

SWELL.

Ah ! she is selling her house, is she ?

BELLA, *chattering.*

Yes, and so I should have to work in the

country, if I staid with her, and that would spoil my hands. It would be a pity to spoil my hands, wouldn't it ?

SWELL, *taking her hand.*

By Jove ! I should think so.

BELLA, *chattering on.*

So, you see, Mrs. Jackman said she should send me to her sister in town.

SWELL, *quickly.*

Ah ! you go to town.

BELLA.

Oh, dear ! that was a slip, too. [*Anxiously*] Are you not going that way ?

SWELL.

Yes.

BELLA.

Oh, dear ! what luck ? We can go together, because, you know, I'm afraid of people I don't know. I don't associate with everybody. You see, when one is pretty—

SWELL,

And when one knows it.

BELLA, *innocently.*

Yes—I mean, no. Oh, dear ! you make me talk such nonsense.

[*Duet may be introduced here for* BELLA *and* SWELL.]

SWELL.

Have you a sweetheart?

BELLA.

None of your business.

SWELL.

By Jove! ye know, with those eyes, ye ought to have many.

BELLA.

I have none.

SWELL, *gallantly.*

By Jove! ye know, I know one.

BELLA, *innocently.*

Oh, dear! do you?

SWELL.

Yes, by Jove! Won't you give me a lock of your hair?

BELLA.

What for?

SWELL.

Why, isn't a lock of your hair a key to your feelings?

BELLA, *laughing.*

No, unless you pull it.

SWELL.

Then let me pull it at once. [*Tries to kiss her, she escapes off R. He comes down front and sings:*

Air: "Up in a Balloon."

Dearest Arabella,
　Meet me at the gate;
Come prepared to stay out
　Kinder sorter late.
Wrap yourself in cotton,
　Like a tooth that aches;
Drink up the molasses
　For to-morrow's cakes.
Eat about a hundred
　Pounds of honeycomb,
With a pint of syrup,
　Just to send it home.
Send to meet the other things
　Sixteen sugar-loaves,
And, by way of spicing,
　Take two little cloves.
Cover with a pound of
　Maple-sugar chips;
Put a stick of candy
　'Twixt your dainty lips;
Then tell Mr. Edison
　To send the bill to me,
And charge you to the nozzle
　With electricitee.
Then if you will pocket
　That piece of chewing-gum,
Warble like a little bird,
　And I will come!   [*Exit.*

DRUM MAJOR *and* SPORTING GENT *enter L.* DRUM MAJOR *heavily bearded, in a fantastic drum-major's dress.* SPORTING GENT *has spurs, a whip, and jockey cap.*

SPORTING GENT, *continuing a story.*

But that is not all, young man. The most astonishing was the last Derby. A most gorgeous start! Flatman got the lead on Freemason, going like wildfire. Pratt followed close with Pretty Polly; just behind was Miss Pocahontas, then Tomahawk. At the second jump, Miss Pocahontas got ahead—you understand.

DRUM MAJOR, *heroically endeavoring to understand.*

Yes, that young lady got a head—well?

SPORTING GENT.

Flatman let her pass. He knew he could beat her with Freemason at the last ditch. At the third fence, Tomahawk struck forward. But Pratt took a fence splendidly.

DRUM MAJOR.

Ah! if he took offense, they had a fight. Who got the tomahawk?

SPORTING GENT.

Oh, no! I mean he got over the fence.

DRUM MAJOR.

Ah! he was the man on the fence.

SPORTING GENT.

The ditch once over, Miss Pocahontas was coming in first, when Flatman jammed the spurs into Freemason's ribs. Chipney understood the danger, and brought up Tomahawk, and then Pratt began to saw at Miss Pocahontas's mouth, and on they went in fine style. Houp! g'lang! [*Makes gestures of riding race.*]

DRUM MAJOR.

I say, look here! Is it to aggravate me that you get off these bloodthirsty stories—though it makes one's blood run cold—about your friend who saws at the young lady's mouth? It's all wrong. You hear! Ah, if I had only been there!

SPORTING GENT.

But, my friend, Miss Pocahontas and Freemason are—

DRUM MAJOR, *forcibly.*

I am one—a freemason—and if any one struck me with a tomahawk, or forced spurs into my ribs—I—I— [*Calmly*] I would complain at headquarters.

SPORTING GENT, *half angry.*

Thick-headed soldier, don't you understand?

DRUM MAJOR, *forcibly*.

I grant you must amuse yourself, flirt with ladies, but cut off their heads with a saw—oh, it is atrocious! degrading! That's my opinion.

SPORTING GENT, *thoroughly angry*.

But, unfortunate wretch, did you never before hear the noble language of the turf?

DRUM MAJOR.

The turf? Stuff! I never ate any! But, if it cause you to act brutally to ladies, I don't want to eat any.

SPORTING GENT, *laughing aside*.

Oh, dear! isn't he green—verdant—refreshing! [*Aloud*] Warrior, you are a bore! What do you take me for? A sanguinary savage, with cannibalistic proclivities? No! I am a member of the Jockey Club, come here for the races. Have you never heard of sport?

DRUM MAJOR, *stupidly*.

Support! Supporting whom?

SPORTING GENT, *angrily*.

I say sport! Sport.

DRUM MAJOR, *calmly*.

No, I never supported anybody.

SPORTING GENT, *angrily.*

Go to the devil, if you can't understand !

DRUM MAJOR.

I understand now.   You wished to aggravate
me.   I shall complain to the Colonel.   [*Pointing
to Burgomaster, who enters L.*]

BURGOMASTER, *coming down C.*

A row here in my diggins !   What the diggins
does it mean ?

DRUM MAJOR.

Colonel, this individual—

BURGOMASTER.

Call me Burgomaster.

DRUM MAJOR.

Yes, Colonel.   You see, this individual—

BURGOMASTER.

Your passports !

DRUM MAJOR.

Here, Colonel.   [*They show them.*]   This individual—

BURGOMASTER.

Your name !

DRUM MAJOR.

Smith, Drum Major of the Ninety-Ninth
Scandinavian Horse Marines.

BURGOMASTER, *excitedly*.

Smith ! Heavens ! That eye ! that mouth ! those nose ! If it were he ! [*To Drum Major*] To my arms !

DRUM MAJOR.

Yes, Colonel. [*Passively falls in Burgomaster's arms.*]

BURGOMASTER.

Dear child ! It was you, was it not, I left on the banks of the Kalbsbratenthaler ?

DRUM MAJOR, *puzzled*.

On the banks of the Kalbsbratenthaler, Colonel.

BURGOMASTER.

Yes ; collect your reminiscences. Do you remember Charley, to whom I lent the money the General gave me ?

DRUM MAJOR.

Oh, the General ! [*Makes military salute.*]

BURGOMASTER.

Charley, the apple-pie man, who used to make you apple pies and tarts.

DRUM MAJOR, *utterly bewildered*.
Pison tarts ?

BURGOMASTER, *excitedly*.

Yes. Remember ! Remember ! Ah, thousand thunders ! he forgets.

SPORTING GENT.

I say, Colonel, you crush my passport in your affectionate anguish. Return it.

BURGOMASTER.

One moment. [*To Drum Major*] Stay here. [*To Sporting Gent*] Your name ?

SPORTING GENT.

Smith !

BURGOMASTER.

Smith ! !

DRUM MAJOR.

Smith ! ! !

BURGOMASTER, *reading.*

Heavens ! 'tis true. That eye ! that mouth ! those nose ! If it were he ! What shall I do ? Only wanted one son. I find three. I faint. [*Faints—Drum Major catches him. Bella and Swell enter R. U. E.*]

Tableau.

BELLA, *to Burgomaster C.*

Do you feel better ?

BURGOMASTER, *waking up.*

Where am I ? [*Looks around.*] Ah, yes ! [*Suddenly takes to striding up and down stage.*] How embarrassing ! Three sons—which to recognize—which to press to my paternal bosom. One thousand conflicting emotions rend my tortured breast, and I have not my boots.

VON B., *entering R.*

Your honor, here is an official telegram.

BURGOMASTER, *bewildered.*

A telegram ! my son—oh, dear !

VON B.

They said it was important. [*Exit R.*

BURGOMASTER, *C.*

Important ! Well, duty after all else. [*Reads*] " Burgomaster Smith, on receipt of this, will scour the country with all available forces, and recapture the riding man-monkey, the Cynocephalus." [*Spoken*] What ! the Cynocephalus has escaped ! How lucky if I recaptured it ! Ah ! there is a P. S. [*Reads*] " He answers to the name of Smith." Thousand thunders ! if he were my son. How embarrassing ! My duty. [*Takes stage R.*]

SPORTING GENT, *follows R. and stands R.*

My passport.

BURGOMASTER.

My affection. [*Takes stage L.*]

SWELL, *follows and stands L.*

My passport.

BURGOMASTER.

My head whirls.   [*Takes stage up R.*]

BELLA, *follows and stands up R.*
My passport.

BURGOMASTER.

The Cynocephalus my son.   [*Takes stage up L.*]

DRUM MAJOR, *follows and stands up L.*
My passport.

BURGOMASTER, *C.*

Leave me alone.   I can't think without my boots.

ALL, *coming C.*
But, Colonel.

BURGOMASTER, *heroically.*

I go to put them on.   [*Exit into house.*

BELLA, *R. C.*

He looks irritated.

SPORTING GENT, *L. C., to her.*
Charming creature !

SWELL *comes C. between them.*

BELLA, *courtesying.*

You are polite, sir.   [*To Drum Major R.*]
What could have caused his emotion ?

DRUM MAJOR, *R.*

Beauteous being, I know not.

SPORTING GENT, *less gallantly.*

One can easily understand that on seeing you he lost his head.

SWELL, *coming again between them.*

By Jove! ye know. Just approach a little farther off.

BELLA, *to Drum Major.*

Perhaps he was ill. Do you know him, sir?

DRUM MAJOR.

Siren, I do not.

BELLA.

But you embraced him.

DRUM MAJOR.

I received the order—I obeyed it. But I should rather have it come from you.

BELLA.

All three of these men seem taken with me. It is a most embarrassing position for a poor maiden.

12

SONG.

Air: Any Waltz.

What can a poor maiden do,
Who is sought by suitors two?
     Or, perhaps, as you see,
     By suitors three,
Who profess, and propose, and pursue.

SWELL.

What can a poor maiden do,
Who is sought by suitors two?
     She had best married be;
     So she should marry me.
To her I will ever be true.

BELLA.

What can a poor maiden do?
She can not cut her heart in two!
     Or love all the three,
     Most affectionatelee!
She can love only one of you.

SPORTING GENT, *repeats stanza sung by* SWELL.

BELLA.

What can a poor maiden do?
The prospect is certainly blue.
     So she had better flee
     To some far countree,
Patagonia, Pekin, or Peru.

DRUM MAJOR *sings stanza sung by* SWELL. *Then all four repeat.*

BELLA, *R.*

Dear me ! it's really very embarrassing.

SWELL.

She sings like an angel.

SPORTING GENT.

She has a pace like a thoroughbred.

DRUM MAJOR.

Your song enchants me, oh, sweetest siren !

BELLA.

Bella is my name, sir—not siren.

DRUM MAJOR.

Yes, my siren.

BELLA.

I say, what is a siren ?

DRUM MAJOR, *puzzled.*

A siren, fair creature—a siren is—

SWELL, *interrupting.*

A woman with a fish's tail.

BELLA.

Oh, dear, how horrid !

DRUM MAJOR.

But, fairest, I assure you.

SPORTING GENT.

You're a bore, if that is your method of making love.

DRUM MAJOR, *angrily*.

You are a nice one, you are, after aggravating me by sawing off a young lady's head, you infuriated vagabond.

SPORTING GENT.

Ruthless wretch !

DRUM MAJOR.

Thousand thunders ! A citizen insults the army. [*Draws sabre.*] Dr-r-r-aw and defend yourself, vile caitiff !

BELLA.

Dear me ! they will kill each other. Help ! murder ! fire !

SWELL.

Ah, here is the Colonel !

BURGOMASTER, *in door of house*.

Wherefore this noise ?

BELLA, *R. to Swell*.

He has his boots.

SWELL, *R. C. to Drum Major*.

He has his boots.

DRUM MAJOR, *L. C. to Sporting Gent.*
He has his boots.

SPORTING GENT, *L. to audience.*
He has his boots.

CHORUS, *all except Burgomaster.*
Air: "Il grandira," from "La Périchole," Offenbach.

He has his boots!
He has his boots!
He has his boots, and he's a man of gore!

BURGOMASTER.

In private life I am a right good fellow—
    At most a very ordinary man.
I play the flute, I play the violoncello,
    And on the drum I do the best I can.
These tastes may cause my fellow men to shun me;
    But still they show a breast unused to war.
Yet now, behold [*repeat*], a change has come upon me;
    I have my boots [*three times*], and I'm a man of gore.
                                    [CHORUS *as before.*

My brain is clear; my cra-ni-um is level;
    I substitute the lion for the lamb.
In blood I bask; in devastation revel;
    And that's the sort of hurricane I am.
No more will I my spirit high dissemble,
    And imitate the clam on ocean's shore.
The world shall shake [*repeat*], the solar system trem-
        ble—
    I have my boots [*three times*], and I'm a man of gore.
                                    [CHORUS *as before.*

BELLA.

I should not like to stand in his shoes when he has those boots on.

BURGOMASTER.

Wherefore this disturbance ?

DRUM MAJOR.

He insulted the army.

SPORTING GENT.

Not at all.   He insulted this lady.

DRUM MAJOR.

I want satisfaction.   Ber-r-r-lud !   A duel !

ALL.

A duel ?

BELLA.

Oh, dear !

BURGOMASTER, *confused.*

A duel.   The Cynocephalus, my son.

DRUM MAJOR.

I am an officer.

SPORTING GENT.

I might have been one.   I will prove it. Colonel, lend me thy sword.

BURGOMASTER, *waking up.*

My sword. [*Looking at Sporting Gent*] Heavens! what do I see? That whip! those spurs! 'tis he! 'tis he!

SPORTING GENT, *aside.*

What does he say?

BURGOMASTER, *to Sporting Gent.*

Your name is Smith?

SPORTING GENT.

Yes.

BURGOMASTER.

I arrest you.

SPORTING GENT.

Arrest me! What for?

BURGOMASTER, *peremptorily.*

Your real name is Cynocephalus. You have escaped from the Royal Senegambian Circus. To prison! [*Aside*] With my boots on, I am astonishingly clever.

SPORTING GENT, *takes R.*

This is an outrage!

SWELL [*lisping*].

By Jove! ye know, you thee what it is to be too gallant.

BURGOMASTER, *hurriedly.*

What do I hear ?   That foreign accent.   'Tis he !   [*To Swell*] Your name is Smith.

SWELL.

Yes.

BURGOMASTER.

I arrest you.

BELLA.

Oh, dear !

SWELL, *angrily.*

Arrest me !   Why ?

BURGOMASTER.

You will be told after.

SWELL.

What right have you to— ?

BURGOMASTER, *grandly.*

By my authority as Burgomaster, I order you to prison, which you will leave [*excitedly*] only to do the Flying Leap of the Bounding Antelope of the Choctaw Desert.

SWELL.

The flying leap.

SPORTING GENT.

The bounding antelope.

BELLA.

The Choctaw Desert.

SWELL.

Sanguinary antiquity, this is an outrage to—

BURGOMASTER, *grandly*.

You resist. Ah, ha! 'tis well. Drum Major, I invoke your assistance. Seize that bloodthirsty ruffian. [*Points to Sporting Gent and takes Swell by collar.*]

SWELL, *struggling feebly*.

Thith ith outrageouth. By Jove! ye know, to arrest a fellow for no offenth.

BURGOMASTER, *with lisp and Swell's accent*.

By Jove! ye know, I know your offenth.

SWELL, *struggling feebly*.

Let me get my thack.

BURGOMASTER.

I'll keep your thack, you thee.

SWELL, *wildly*.

He taketh my thack; he taketh my accent; he taketh me by the collar; he hath a very taking way.

BURGOMASTER.

It aggravates him to be taken off, poor little fellow.

SWELL, *struggling*.

Don't pull my collar.

BURGOMASTER.

Don't be choleric. [*Pulls him into house where Drum Major has put Sport, and locks door.*]

DRUM MAJOR.

Ah, Colonel! I think I was of great assistance.

BURGOMASTER, *calmly.*

Drum Major, I am satisfied with your conduct on this memorable and glorious, though sanguinary, occasion. [*Suddenly regarding Drum Major.*] Ah! what do I see? Ah! [*Jumps wildly.*] The monkey-man is bearded. This hair. [*Pointing to Drum Major.*] He answers to the name of Smith. [*To Drum Major*] Cynocephalus, I arrest you.

DRUM MAJOR, *astonished.*

How, Cynocephalus! I do not know that individual. He is not in my regiment.

BURGOMASTER, *authoritatively.*

I arrest you—you are a leapist.

DRUM MAJOR, *astonished.*

But, Colonel.

BURGOMASTER.

You resist? Ah, ha! to prison. [*Crosses L.*]

DRUM MAJOR.

But I am the Drum Major of the Ninety-ninth Scandinavian Horse Marines.

BURGOMASTER.

No observations ! [*Pushes him into house, locks door, and comes down R.*] At last.

BELLA.

Oh, dear ! Poor young man !

BURGOMASTER, *sagely to Bella.*

Female peasantess, your name is Smith ?

BELLA.

Bella Smith, your honor.

BURGOMASTER, *aside.*

Ha, ha ! This is suspicious. We must cross-question her. [*Aloud*] So you pretend to be a girl ?

BELLA.

Yes, your honor.

BURGOMASTER.

Call me Colonel.

BELLA.

Yes, your honor. What have these poor young men done, to be locked up ?

BURGOMASTER, *inquisitionally*.

You are going to the railroad ?

BELLA.

Yes, your honor.

BURGOMASTER, *roughly*.

Call me Colonel.

BELLA.

Yes, your honor.   Why did you arrest them ?
It is perfectly ridiculous.

BURGOMASTER, *dignified*.

Female peasantess !

BELLA.

Oh, dear ! it was a slip.   Is it because they
would not be your sons ?

BURGOMASTER, *grandly*.

They are my sons no longer.

BELLA.

Who are they then ?

BURGOMASTER, *wildly*.

Who are they ?   [*Calmly*] The Cynocephalus.

BELLA.

Oh, dear !   Which ?

Burgomaster.

All three.

Bella.

That is utterly idiotic.

Burgomaster, *severely.*

Female peasantess !

Bella.

It was a slip. [*Coaxingly*] Your honor, they have done nothing to you. Let me have one— the little one. He fell in love with me.

Burgomaster, *with the air of Brutus.*

His name is Smith.

Bella.

Is that a reason ? Mine is Smith, too. Why not arrest me ?

Burgomaster, *sagely.*

I thought of it. [*Takes snuff.*]

Bella.

Just what I should have expected from you.

Burgomaster, *dignified.*

Female peasantess !

Bella.

It was a slip. [*Very coaxingly*] But, you

dear, good, kind, nice old general, let me have the little one, please.

BURGOMASTER, *inexorable.*

His name is Smith.

BELLA, *quickly.* .

So is yours.

BURGOMASTER, *startled.*

So it is!' Heavens! I had forgotten. What shall I do? The orders are plain. Perhaps I am the Cynocephalus.

BELLA, *watching him, aside.*

Oh, dear! What is the matter with him now?

BURGOMASTER, *down R.*

An old soldier should suffer without complaining. I must incarcerate myself. [*Goes majestically to door L. and solemnly returns to Bella down L. C.*] [*Suspiciously*] You are sure you are a girl?

BELLA, *angrily.*

Colonel, you are an impolite old boy! I am disgusted, astonished, and astounded!

BURGOMASTER, *sagely, aside.*

Such mildness. She must be a girl.

[*Exit into house. Lights down.*

BELLA.

Oh, dear! how disagreeable. He might have left me one—the little one. The devastating old reprobate. And how dark it is all at once!

SWELL, on balcony, Sporting Gent and Drum Major behind him.

Psth! Psth!

BELLA, *looking up.*

Ah! there he is. [*To Swell*] The Burgomaster has gone inside.

SWELL.

Hush! Speak lower. We will escape by this window.

BELLA.

How?

SWELL.

By means of that ladder, which I see there. [*Points R.*]

BELLA.

All right. [*Sets it at side of house.*]

SWELL.

By Jove! ye know, it is dangerous; but I shall risk it. Hold firm! [*Aside to audience*] Sensation! [*He descends ladder calmly—music tremolo.*]

BELLA.

Heavens, this is frightful! [*Drum Major and Sporting Gent descend. Music crescendo.*]

BELLA.

Saved !   Saved at last !

ALL.

Saved !   [*Burlesque sensation tableau.*]

SPORTING GENT.

Now to escape.

BELLA, *up C.*

Yes—

DRUM MAJOR, *R.*

We—

SWELL, *C.*

Must—

SPORTING GENT, *L.*

Escape—

QUARTET.

BELLA.

Now this is really trying :
The time has come for flying ;
But day is slowly dying,
        And we shall be in the dark.

SWELL.

Let each one stick to the other,
As though he were his brother,
And never make any bother,
        While we are in the dark.

[CHORUS, *repeat first stanza.*

SPORTING GENT.

Without running, jumping, leaping,
But softly, gently creeping,
While all the world is sleeping,
    We steal away in the dark.

           [CHORUS *as before.*

DRUM MAJOR.

Ere we can sing a ditty,
We must be out of the city,
Away from this maiden pretty,
    Alone here in the dark!

[CHORUS *as before, ending in short, mysterious dance.*

SWELL, *L. C.*

When does the first train pass?

SPORTING GENT.

I have my paper in my pocket [*takes out paper*], but I can't see. [*To prompter, off stage*]. Turn up the gas a little, please. [*Lights up.*] Thank you.

SWELL.

The latest from the seat of war.

ALL, *anxiously.*

Ah!

SPORTING GENT.

No news.

SWELL, *looking on paper, starting.*

Ah!

13

ALL.

What ?

SWELL.

Here.

ALL.

Yes.

SWELL.

See ! [*Pointing to paper.*]

ALL.

Well ?

SWELL, *reads.*

"Information wanted of a Mr. Smith, who was Colonel of the Hackendrackenstackenfelstein Mounted Fire Extinguishers, who in 1832 lent money to one Charley, the apple-pie man."

BELLA.

The Burgomaster.

SWELL.

Listen ! "The said Charley, being a widow, died, leaving a fortune of thirty-two millions to the said Smith."

ALL.

Thirty-two millions.   Oh !

BELLA.

You lose time ; you must fly.

SWELL.

True.   [*Aside, going*] And he took me for his son.

SPORTING GENT, *aside.*

After all, he may be my father.

DRUM MAJOR, *aside.*

Since he is my superior, and he says he is my father—

BELLA, *looking in house L.*

He comes. Hide.

ALL.

Yes.   [*Enter inn R.*

VON B. *enters R., goes L.*

VON B.

Your honor, another telegram.

BURGOMASTER, *inside.*

What is it ?

VON B.

An official telegram.

BURGOMASTER, *at door, taking it.*

Heavens ! [*von B. exits.*] "The Cynocephalus was recaptured this morning in the spire of
Trinity Church." [*Comes down C.*] Then I am
free. These young persons are innocent.

BELLA, *aside.*

Oh, dear ! I hope he won't perceive their
flight.

BURGOMASTER.

They must be released.

SWELL, *at the door of inn, overhearing, aside.*
Release us.

BURGOMASTER, *turning, sees him.*
What do I see ?

BELLA, *aside.*
How imprudent!

SWELL, *coming down, followed by Sporting Gent
and Drum Major.*
Yes, it is I. I had escaped. I was wrong.
I would not injure a noble Burgomaster. I return. Arrest me.

DRUM MAJOR, *heroically.*
Me.

SPORTING GENT, *nobly.*
And me.

BURGOMASTER, *explaining.*
But—

SWELL.
I shall obey you as a father.

BURGOMASTER, *rapturously.*
A father !

DRUM MAJOR.
Colonel, you also called me your son.

BURGOMASTER.

How embarrassing! What shall I do?

BELLA.

Perhaps they are all your sons.

SWELL, SPORTING GENT, and DRUM MAJOR.

Father! [*Kneeling.*]

Tableau.

BURGOMASTER.

Oh, my heart is distracted! My sons in my arms—all three. [*He embraces them all.*]

BELLA.

Oh, dear! this is affecting.

BURGOMASTER, *rejecting them severely.*

Now tell me why you left the tree where I placed you?

DRUM MAJOR, *dubiously.*

The tree?

SPORTING GENT, *inquiringly.*

The tree?

SWELL, *wildly.*

The tree?

BELLA.

They have forgotten.

BURGOMASTER.

True, it was long ago. [*Suddenly*] Do you remember your great-aunt, Amethystenella Smith?

BELLA, *surprised, coming down.*

Amethystenella was my mother. [*Chord.*

ALL.

Ah !

BELLA.

Yes. As a proof of it, here is her cross.

ALL.

Ah ! her mother's cross.

BELLA.

And here are her papers.

BURGOMASTER.

Can she be my niece? [*Trying to read papers.*] I can't read with my boots on. [*To Swell*] Read !

SWELL.

Yes. [*Reads.*] Ha ! Thith ith hith aunt.

SPORTING GENT, *lisps.*

Hith aunt.

DRUM MAJOR, *lisps.*

Hith aunt.

BELLA, *lisps.*

Hith aunt.

CHORUS.

Air : " He has his boots."

This is his aunt, [*three times*] he never knew before.

BURGOMASTER.

Ith is my aunt.

BELLA.

Yes, your aunt. Only what I regret is, you did not find it out before, as now you may think I recognize you on account of your fortune.

BURGOMASTER, *astonished.*

My fortune.

DRUM MAJOR.

Yes. Charley has died and left you thirty-two millions.

BURGOMASTER.

Charley dead ! Poor old fellow ! Ah ! my sons, I adopt you all ; you must never leave me.

SWELL, SPORTING GENT, and DRUM MAJOR.
We won't.

BURGOMASTER, *confidentially.*

We ought to have a wedding to end up.

SWELL, *L. C., taking Bella's hand.*
We will see to that. [*To Bella, L.*] Won't we, dearest ?

BELLA.
Yes, ducky.

MR. *and* MRS. VON B. *enter R.*

MR. VON B.
Our married life begins anew.

MRS. VON B.
Yes, we've agreed to disagree.

BURGOMASTER.
All right, now we only need a little music to end.

MUSICAL FINALE.
Air: " Yankee Doodle."

BURGOMASTER, *R. C.*

To sing a song is never wrong,
    And so we'll have a chorus.
Your stay with us we'll not prolong,
    O friends we see before us.

ALL, *repeat as chorus.*
To sing a song, etc.

SWELL, *L. C.*

Put on your shawls!   These mimic halls
    Will soon be very lonely.
We ask, before the curtain falls,
    Your approbation only.

ALL, *repeat as chorus.*
To sing a song, etc.

BELLA, *C.*
Here we all stand, a timid band,
  We can not now dissemble;
Until you give what we demand,
  We shiver, shake, and tremble.

ALL, *repeat as chorus.*
To sing a song, etc.

CURTAIN.

FRANK WYLDE.

COMEDY IN ONE ACT.

By J. BRANDER MATTHEWS.

CHARACTERS.

FRANK WYLDE.

CAPTAIN CULPEPPER COLDSPRING, *of Rio Janeiro, Brazil.*

MRS. JULIET MONTAGUE, *his niece.*

ROSE, *her maid.*

[The French original of this play is " *Le Serment d'Horace,*" written by M. Henry Mürger.]

FRANK WYLDE.

SCENE : A handsome parlor. Doors C., R. 2 E., and L. 1 E. Fireplace L. 2 E. Clock and handsome vases on mantelpiece L. 2 E. Table R., with books, two cheap china vases, and Mrs. Montague's photograph neatly framed. Piano L. C., with two cheap china vases on it. Mrs. Montague's miniature on wall R. Sofa before fire C. Folded screens at back L. C.

Rose discovered, lighting gas.

ROSE.

Well, I must say that I like these apartment houses better than a horrid hotel. French flats they call 'em. I don't think the French are flats at all if they invented these houses and cooking, and the fashions besides. [*Clock on mantel strikes eight.*] Eight! She must be done dinner by this time! Ah! Here she is!

MRS. JULIET MONTAGUE, *entering D. C.*
Rose !.

ROSE.

Yes, ma'am.

MRS. MONTAGUE, *languidly.*

Bring me a chair by the fire ! Not that one.
An arm-chair.

ROSE.

Here, ma'am. [*Putting arm-chair before fire.*]

MRS. MONTAGUE.

Those elevators are always so cold. [*Sits and
warms her feet.*] Has the Captain come in yet ?

ROSE.

No, ma'am.

CAPTAIN CULPEPPER COLDSPRING *throws open
D. C., rushes in violently, very angry.*

The devil take New York and the New-Yorkers. They're a pack of ninnies ! fools ! [*Shouting*] Idiots !

ROSE, *hurriedly, bringing vase from piano.*

Here, sir ! [*Captain smashes it angrily on
floor, and rushes off, banging door L. 1 E.*]
[*Frightened*] Ah !

MRS. MONTAGUE, *very calmly, glancing at herself
in a mirror.*

Well, Rose, what's the matter ?

ROSE.

I shall never get used to the Captain, ma'am.
He's very savage.

MRS. MONTAGUE.

I suppose he has been quarreling. [*Calmly*]
I hope he has not killed anybody. Gather up the
fragments, Rose ; put them with the others !
[*Rose picks up bits of china vase, and throws them
in basket behind fireplace L. 2 E.*] And in case
his wrath is not yet assuaged, have another fire-
escape—safety-valve—lightning-rod ready for him!

CAPTAIN, *off L.*

Rose ! [*Entering L. 1 E.*] Rose !

ROSE, *going for another vase.*

Sir ?

CAPTAIN.

Lay to !

ROSE, *surprised.*

Lay to ?

CAPTAIN, *sharply.*

Lay to !

ROSE.

But, sir—I—

CAPTAIN.

Stop !

ROSE.

Ah ! I see ! Never having navigated, sir, I
didn't know. After this I'll lay to !

CAPTAIN.

Shut up! I don't like your voice! Get another organ or I'll discharge you!

ROSE.

But, sir, indeed, I—

CAPTAIN.

Silence! Take this money and give it to that waiter of Delmonico's outside! [*Shouting*] Why don't you go? [*Rose jumps, frightened, and exit C.*] That girl irritates my nerves! [*About to take vase from mantelpiece.*]

MRS. MONTAGUE, *calmly*.

Excuse me, uncle, one of these. [*Pointing to cheap vases on table.*] If it's the same to you?

CAPTAIN.

I have no preference! Besides, I am calm now.

MRS. MONTAGUE, *tranquilly*.

What has happened? I am all anxiety.

CAPTAIN, *warming his coat-tails at fire*.

Nothing much! only this, in fact. I was puffing a Partaga on Broadway, and I met Pacheco Gomez; you remember Gomez? Eh? Not a bad fellow at all, for a greaser; they hung him three times in Paraguay during Lopez's day.

MRS. MONTAGUE.

Is he well ?

CAPTAIN.

Bad cold. "Coldspring!" said he. "Gomez!" said I. "Yes!" said he. "Come and dine!" said I. And so we walked into Delmonico's and had a good dinner, except the fish, too old, and the sherry, too young. I call for the bill and wait ten, fifteen, twenty minutes, by the watch. At last the bill comes.

MRS. MONTAGUE, *calmly*.

Yes ?

CAPTAIN.

But it was not for me, but for a gentleman who dined near us. I told him very politely that I had asked for my bill before him, and I forbade his paying before me or I would break a bottle on his head.

MRS. MONTAGUE, *tranquilly*.

Well ?

CAPTAIN.

Well, he pays, and I present him with a bottle of claret, on the head, Chateau Margaux, '49.

MRS. MONTAGUE.

You killed him ?

CAPTAIN.

Good claret never hurt anybody. He returned my favor by a Duc de Montebello, extra sec. A

14

battle is waged in the Champagne country.   Row,
shouts, everything topsy-turvy.   The waiters
rush in.   Gomez and I seize two slaves and hurl
them through the window.   General astonish-
ment.   Row ; police ; smash—dinner, $25 ; other
luxuries, $80 ; total, $105.   Things are so dear
in New York.   Ah ! Juliet, you had better come
back to Brazil.

MRS. MONTAGUE.

Never again !   I love New York.

CAPTAIN, *throwing himself on sofa by Mrs. Montague.*

Then acknowledge that I'm a pretty good spe-
cimen of an uncle.   Your old husband exploring
the Pampas is bitten by a snake : in twelve minutes you are a widow ; in twelve days you are con-
soled.

MRS. MONTAGUE.

Oh, uncle !   Oh !

CAPTAIN.

My dear, we are alone !   You curbed your
sorrow carefully, I can certify.

MRS. MONTAGUE.

I assure you—

CAPTAIN.

You wept for your husband twelve days ; you
might have finished the fortnight ; you didn't—

that's your lookout. On the thirteenth day you cried, "I am free, dear uncle, good uncle, kind uncle; I want to see New York." And here we are!

MRS. MONTAGUE, *kissing him.*

You dear, good, kind old uncle!

CAPTAIN.

Exactly. For you I have abandoned my adopted country, my dear Brazil. And to think you could give me back all this—all that I have given up.

MRS. MONTAGUE.

How?

CAPTAIN.

Remarry! Try Cuttyback!

MRS. MONTAGUE, *rising.*

A commonplace commission-merchant! Never! Besides, I don't like Mr. Cuttyback!

CAPTAIN.

He is rich, and yet young—only thirty-two. The mean of human life is thirty-three. Cuttyback has only one year more. In another year you are again a widow. That don't matter; you make a jolly little widow!

MRS. MONTAGUE.

Uncle, you are a wretch!

CAPTAIN.

If Cuttyback is not amenable to these statistics, just return to Brazil; inoculate him with a taste for botany; he wanders o'er the Pampas, and then—pop! The happy serpent that made you a widow has probably brought up a struggling family.

MRS. MONTAGUE.

Uncle, you are atrocious!

CAPTAIN, *toasting his feet and chuckling.*

Ha! ha! I must have my joke. Poor Cuttyback! Josiah Cuttyback! Has he been courting to-day?

MRS. MONTAGUE.

No!

CAPTAIN.

Perhaps he forgot it, he is so absent-minded. Perhaps he called while you were out. Rose! Rose!

ROSE, *entering C.*

Sir?

CAPTAIN.

Has Mr. Cuttyback called to-day?

ROSE.

No, sir.

CAPTAIN.

He forgot it. Absent-minded Cuttyback! [*Takes his hat.*]

MRS. MONTAGUE.

Are you going out ?

CAPTAIN.

For a minute only. Gomez and I are going
to have a Mocha and a fire-water together at the
Hoffmann. Ah ! By the by, Rose, have they
brought my coat ?

ROSE.

Not yet, sir.

CAPTAIN.

If the tailor comes, tell him to wait. [*Angrily*] Do you hear ?

ROSE, *jumping*.

Yes, sir ; of course.

CAPTAIN.

These servants are so stupid. In Brazil, where
they are black, you can sell them. But she is
white. You have not the right.

ROSE.

That's a very good thing !

CAPTAIN.

This girl—this Rose, now, is insupportable.
Now, if she were only black, she'd bring a thousand dollars.

ROSE, *indignantly*.

A thousand dollars, indeed ! I should think so !

CAPTAIN.

Let's see your teeth. Whew! Perhaps twelve
hundred. But she's white. You haven't the
right.   [*Puts on hat and exit C.*

ROSE.

What a tiger!

MRS. MONTAGUE, *rising languidly.*

My uncle goes out very often. [*Sighs.*] I'll
try the piano. [*Plays a few notes, then rises.*]
Oh, it's false! It wants tuning—so do I. [*Sits
on sofa.*] Rose, I'm very bored. Do you know
what *ennui* is?

ROSE.

Yes, ma'am ; it's a French word.

MRS. MONTAGUE.

Rose!

ROSE.

Ma'am?

MRS. MONTAGUE.

Tell me a fairy story. [*Yawns and leans back.*]

ROSE, *laughing.*

Certainly, ma'am. "Once upon a time there
was a beautiful princess, who was a widow, and
beautiful—oh, so beautiful!—as beautiful as
Cleopatrick. One day, coming from the bath,
she saw Prince Charming—oh, so handsome!

so young ! only eighteen—and such a lovely mustache."

MRS. MONTAGUE.

Your tale is false, Rose. Prince Charming was a commission-merchant in Pearl Street, and his name was Josiah Cuttyback. [*Bell rings.*] There he is now. Let him in.

ROSE, *sighing.*

Yes, ma'am. [*Exit C.*

MRS. MONTAGUE.

He comes in the nick of time. I shall proceed to make him miserable. All men like being made miserable, and then it may amuse me. [*Rose enters C., with a card on a salver.*] Ask him in, Rose.

ROSE.

Yes, ma'am—but it's not Mr. Cuttyback.

MRS. MONTAGUE.

Indeed !

ROSE.

He sent in his card.

MRS. MONTAGUE, *reading.*

"Mr. Frank Wylde." I don't know him. But perhaps he is some friend of uncle's. Ask him in.

ROSE *goes to door C., and admits* FRANK

WYLDE, *who has a light overcoat over his arm and a note-book in his hand.*

FRANK, *bowing.*

Pray excuse the intrusion, madam.

ROSE, *aside.*

I know it's him !   [*Exit C.*

FRANK.

I have the honor of addressing [*looking in note-book*] Mrs. Juliet Montague ?

MRS. MONTAGUE.

Yes, sir.

FRANK.

Haight House, second floor, number two ?

MRS. MONTAGUE.

Yes, sir.   [*Aside*] This is rather odd.

FRANK *pockets note-book, and, drawing white pocket-handkerchief from his pocket, spreads it on the carpet and kneels.*

FRANK.

Very well.   All right so far.   Madam, I have the honor of offering you my hand and heart.

MRS. MONTAGUE, *rising in surprise.*

Your hand ?

FRANK.

And heart. Both. I know you're going to say you don't know me. True, I don't know you either. You see, if we knew each other, it would no longer be fun.

MRS. MONTAGUE, *very calmly.*

A lunatic, an escaped madman, in my room !

FRANK, *trying to start conversation.*

You see, madam, I—

MRS. MONTAGUE, *pointing to door.*

Leave me instantly, sir !

FRANK.

But—

MRS. MONTAGUE *touches bell on table. Rose enters C.*

Show Mr.— Show this gentleman to the door.

ROSE.

Yes, ma'am.

FRANK.

The deuce !   [*Exit C., bowing profusely.*

MRS. MONTAGUE *thinks a moment, and then laughs.*

Ah ! ah ! There's a way of proposing ! "I have the honor of offering you my hand and heart."

Ah! ah! How comic! I ought to have let this eccentric being remain. He might have amused me.

FRANK, *entering quickly C.*

He asks nothing better, madam. Let us have the kindness to be seated.

MRS. MONTAGUE.

But, sir, to whom have I the honor of speaking?

FRANK.

Certainly. Mr. Frank Wylde. [*Bows, draws up a chair, and sits.*] Frank Wylde, by name and nature. My friends say I'm frank, and my most intimate enemies say I'm wild. My age—a certain age. I have arrived at years of indiscretion. My weight—one hundred and thirty-three in the shade. My fortune—twenty thousand a year. My profession [*sadly*]—unfortunate!

MRS. MONTAGUE.

You have a lucrative practice.

FRANK, *confidentially.*

I'm a gentleman of elegant leisure. My father, unfortunately, left me a fortune, and I have nothing to do except to spend money and time; and I find it very hard work indeed. Do you know, I think a man that has nothing to do is a nuisance to his friends and himself—at least, I find it so.

MRS. MONTAGUE.

So do I.

FRANK.

I am glad you agree with me. Yes, madam, my life is very monotonous. I get up—I breakfast—I read the papers. Nothing new, of course. I drive—I dine—I go to the club or the theatre; perhaps I have supper. I go to bed—I sleep— and the next day [*tragically*]—the next day I begin again !

MRS. MONTAGUE.

I sympathize with you.

FRANK.

Thank you, madam. You see, having nothing to do, I naturally want to do something— anything ! everything ! Riding as I do in the Fifth Avenue omnibus of monotony, I need novelty. I thirst for novelty ! I die for novelty ! [*Looking at his watch.*] Please pay attention, madam. I can give you only four minutes more. Listen ! I was at a reception yesterday; I left early, and took the wrong overcoat by mistake, and in the pocket I found the novelty.

MRS. MONTAGUE.

Indeed !

FRANK.

Yes, madam. I found the long-sought novelty, bound in Russian leather. 'Tis here. [*Showing note-book.*]

MRS. MONTAGUE, *reading.*

"Cuttyback!"

FRANK.

Josiah Cuttyback, a commission-merchant, an absent-minded gentleman, too, for he has written over night all his intentions for the next day.

MRS. MONTAGUE.

Ah! Ah! I see!

FRANK.

Madam, you are perspicacious. My life bored me. I said : "Suppose I try Cuttyback's life? I have nothing to do. Suppose I do what Cuttyback has to do?" Here is the programme of his day's work—I have sworn to follow it faithfully. [*Opens note-book.*]

MRS. MONTAGUE.

I confess my curiosity.

FRANK.

"First : Buy 40 bags Java coffee and 75 barrels sugar." It is done. You may well say it is too much for a bachelor, but my morning coffee is assured for the rest of my life. It is done. I erase. "Second : At 7.30 P. M. offer Mrs. Juliet

Montague, Haight House, second floor, number two, my hand and heart." I beg you to remember that at exactly thirty minutes past seven I suspended myself on your door-bell. "Third: Don't stand any nonsense from the uncle, old Culpepper! If necessary, be disrespectful!" This paragraph is illustrated.

MRS. MONTAGUE.

Illustrated! How?

FRANK.

A horizontal leg is directed toward a gentleman looking the other way. A dangerous paragraph, not fulfilled yet. I do not erase.

MRS. MONTAGUE.

What, sir! Would you dare?

FRANK.

Madam, I have sworn a solemn oath! Lastly —"Fourth: At eight o'clock, take a Turkish bath. Remember and have Mustapha rub me down." [*Rising*] Gracious heavens! Is your clock right?

MRS. MONTAGUE.

Yes, sir.

FRANK.

Eight o'clock! Excoriated at the idea of leaving you, madam—but duty calls. "I go, but I return!"

MRS. MONTAGUE.

That will be unnecessary, sir.   If this is a wager, you have won it.

FRANK.

It is not a wager, madam—it is an oath I swore.   I obey.   I return.   Mustapha must not be kept waiting.   The purification completed, I return.

MRS. MONTAGUE.

No, sir.   Never again !

FRANK.

I go, but I return.   [*Exit C.*

MRS. MONTAGUE.

He's a lunatic.   And here my uncle leaves me exposed to— [*Laughs*] Ah ! ah ! Decidedly, he is eccentric.   "I go, but I return."   I hope he will not, and yet— [*Rings bell.*]

ROSE, *entering C.*

You rang, ma'am ?

MRS. MONTAGUE.

Open the windows here !   The room is close ! [*Bell heard.*]   There's Mr. Cuttyback !

ROSE.

Shall I ask him in ?

Mrs. Montague.

N—no. Say Mrs. Montague is not very well, and desires to be excused.

[*Exit R. 2 E., bell rings furiously.*

Rose, *going to door C.*

Cuttyback is in a hurry. [*Opens door C.*]

Frank, *rushing in quickly.*

I am furious ! Mustapha had gone to Kalybia —to Ujiji—to look for Stanley, and will not be back for a year. Too bad ! [*Looks around.*] Why ! where is she ? Well, I like that ! She knew I was coming back, and yet she does not remain ! Some people really have no idea of *savoir faire* or *savoir vivre.*

Rose, *aside.*

I'm sure it is he ! [*Aloud*] Mr. Frank !

Frank.

My name !

Rose.

Don't you recognize me ? I am Rose.

Frank.

Rose ! What Rose ?

Rose.

I used to be lady's maid to Miss Montmorency.

FRANK.

Ah, yes! [*Changing tone*] What Montmorency?

ROSE.

Miss Mary Montmorency, the prima donna who used to live in Bleecker Street!

FRANK.

Ah, yes! of course; but, Rose, you will understand that I scarcely wish to discuss such a subject as Miss Montmorency of Bleecker Street, now, at the present time, when I offer Mrs. Montague my heart and hand.

ROSE.

You're going to marry her?

FRANK.

Marry her? [*Looks in note-book.*] No, I think not—no. I only offered her my hand and heart. That's all.

ROSE.

Why not marry her? She's a widow.

FRANK.

Oh, ho! It's a second edition, then! [*Looks at miniature.*] Who's that?

ROSE.

That's her portrait.

FRANK, *taking it.*

Per bacco! she's pretty—very pretty—quite pretty! I had not noticed her! [*Pockets miniature.*]

ROSE.

Mr. Frank, you mustn't take it!

FRANK.

Why not? I'll send back the frame.

ROSE.

Oh, no, Mr. Frank; give it back at once!

FRANK, *not minding her.*

Rose, who's this? [*Takes photograph.*]

ROSE.

That's her, too.

FRANK.

Indeed! Her photo. You don't say! Why, she's an angel! a houri! [*Pockets photograph.*]

" O woman, in our hours of ease,
    Uncertain, coy, and hard to please,
    Yet seen too oft, familiar with her face,
    We first endure, then pity, then embrace! "

ROSE.

Please give it back!

FRANK.

I'll return the frame!

15

ROSE.

But, Mr. Frank—

FRANK.

Don't bother ! it isn't yours !

ROSE.

That's true.   It's her lookout, not mine. [*Turns up L.*]   Why, they've let the fire out.

FRANK.

Are you cold ?   [*Kisses her.*]

ROSE.

Oh !

FRANK.

I've struck a light !

CAPTAIN, *rushing in C.*

The devil take New York and the New-Yorkers.   They're a pack of fools ! ninnies ! idiots ! [*Shouting*]   Idiots !

ROSE, *bringing vase.*

Here you are, sir !

CAPTAIN, *smashing it.*

Bang !   Ah !   I feel better.   [*Exit L. 1 E.*

FRANK.

Who is this typhoon ?

ROSE.

It's old Culpepper—her uncle.

[*Exit C. with broken vase.*

FRANK.

Old Culpepper—her uncle! The illustrated paragraph! *Per bacco!* it won't be so easy.

CAPTAIN, *entering L.*

Here, Rose, take this fifty-dollar bill! I say! is there nobody here? [*Throws his cigar-stump on Frank's feet.*]

FRANK.

Look out, there!

CAPTAIN.

You're a nuisance! Go away! Can you understand a simple story?

FRANK.

I think so, if it's very simple.

CAPTAIN.

I was in the café of Delmonico's. Some fellows were talking about shooting and their skill. It annoyed me.

FRANK.

Why?

CAPTAIN.

Don't be so inquisitive! It annoyed me, I say! I drew this revolver from my pocket—

FRANK, *uneasy*.

I say, there, it isn't loaded ?

CAPTAIN.

Oh, yes, one barrel !

FRANK.

That's enough.

CAPTAIN.

When the waiter brought me a light for my cigar—bang ! I snuff it at twenty paces.

FRANK.

Ah, ha ! And you killed a mirror !

CAPTAIN.

Dead ! Fifty dollars. How dear things are in New York. Rose ! Rose ! That girl will never come ! [*Puts revolver on piano and pulls bell-cord—it breaks.*] Rose !

FRANK.

Let me help you. Rose ! Rose !

CAPTAIN.

Oh, these servants !

FRANK.

Horrible ! aren't they ?

BOTH, *going up C.*

Rose! Rose! Rose!

FRANK.

You're lively. You are—

CAPTAIN.

No, I am calm.

FRANK.

Ah! Yes!

CAPTAIN.

I only get wrathy for sanitary reasons. If I was calm for more than a quarter of an hour, I should fear a stroke of apoplexy. [*Anxiously*] Am I red?

FRANK.

Very!

CAPTAIN.

That girl will be the death of me! Rose! [*Bangs table.*]

FRANK.

Rose! [*Aside*] From a cursory examination I should say his character was a cheerful compound of cayenne and curry! [*Aloud*] Rose! Rose! Ah! an idea! [*Fires revolver up chimney.*]

ROSE, *entering C.*

You rang, sir?

CAPTAIN.

Ah! Ah! That's an idea! Thank you!

FRANK.

Don't mention it. [*They shake hands.*]

CAPTAIN.

Rose, give this money to that waiter.

ROSE.

Yes, sir.   [*Exit C.*

CAPTAIN.

Ah! That's better! Now I have a quarter
of an hour to be amiable.

FRANK.

Ah! Ah! [*Aside*] He is amiable, and the
pistol is not loaded. Now is the time for Paragraph Four. [*Shakes his leg.*]

CAPTAIN.

What's the matter with your leg ?   Eh ?

FRANK.

I'm a little like you—nervous ! [*Captain re-
loads pistol.*] I say ! what are you doing ?

CAPTAIN.

I always keep it loaded—for contingencies !

FRANK, *aside.*

It won't be so easy, after all. I prefer not to
be a contingency.

MRS. MONTAGUE, *entering R.*

Good evening, uncle. [*Sees Frank bow, laughs.*] Ah! Ah! You here still, sir?

FRANK.

Yes, madam, I—

MRS. MONTAGUE.

Indeed, this persistence is peculiar! What do you want? I do not know you.

FRANK, *bowing.*

No!

CAPTAIN.

You don't know him? I don't, either. Ah! Ah! Here I've been talking to him for half an hour.

MRS. MONTAGUE.

He is a gentleman who offers me his hand and heart.

CAPTAIN.

Indeed!

ROSE *enters C.*

FRANK, *bowing.*

Yours truly, Frank Wylde.

CAPTAIN.

But he is laughing at us. Rose, you are a maid of all work; throw this gentleman out of the window!

ROSE.

Oh, sir !

FRANK.

Oh, sir !

MRS. MONTAGUE, *coldly*.

Rose, Mr. Wylde's hat.

FRANK.

Certainly, madam, but under these altered circumstances I have no longer the right to keep anything that belongs to you—here is your portrait.

CAPTAIN.

Your portrait !

MRS. MONTAGUE.

But, sir—

FRANK.

I had taken it.

CAPTAIN.

Why ?

FRANK.

To keep it. Here's your photograph, too. Please excuse me. I have executed every paragraph, except one, and that was only owing to unforeseen circumstances beyond my control. I have done my best, at least. Here is Mr. Cuttyback's note-book ! [*Mrs. Montague takes it.*]

CAPTAIN.

Cuttyback ! I don't understand !

FRANK.

That's unnecessary. Good-by, madam. I hope your future but absent-minded husband will not forget to make you happy.

MRS. MONTAGUE.

He will not, if he carries out Paragraph Five!

FRANK.

Excuse me, there is no Paragraph Five!

MRS. MONTAGUE.

There is—over the page. It is indispensable!

FRANK, *anxiously.*

What is it, madam?

MRS. MONTAGUE.

You should have turned the leaf. [*Pockets note-book.*]

ROSE, *who has read over Mrs. Montague's shoulder, aside.*

Ah! Ah! I see!

MRS. MONTAGUE.

Rose, show Mr. Wylde out!

ROSE.

Yes, ma'am. [*Aside*] Ah! Ah! That's a good joke!

FRANK, *discouraged.*

What can it be ?

CAPTAIN, *furiously.*

Are you going ?

FRANK.

Ah ! your quarter of an hour is up ?   Well, I also am wrathy ! enraged ! furious !

CAPTAIN.

Egad, sir !

FRANK.

Egad, sir !

CAPTAIN.

Thousand thunders !

FRANK.

Certainly, thousand thunders !   Paragraph Five.   I shall find it, sooner or later.   In an era when telegraphs, telephones, and railroads have been invented, I at least can discover a paltry Paragraph Five.   I must find it !   [*Taking and smashing vase.*]   Ah !   That's better.   [*To Captain*]   You are right !   It does relieve one's feelings.

CAPTAIN, *threatening.*

Will you go ?   Thousand thunders !

FRANK.

I will go !   Two thousand thunders !   Rose, show me out !   [*Exit C. with Rose.*

CAPTAIN, *furious.*

Thousand thunders! [*Calmly*] I like that
fellow. What is it all about?

MRS. MONTAGUE.

Merely this: That fellow found Mr. Cuttyback's note-book, in which he had written his
work for the day—

CAPTAIN.

Well?

MRS. MONTAGUE.

And that fellow swore to carry out Mr. Cuttyback's programme.

CAPTAIN.

Indeed? Let us be on our guard. [*Rose enters C.*] Perhaps he is a sneak-thief!

ROSE.

Mr. Frank? Oh, dear, no! He is rich and
generous!

MRS. MONTAGUE.

Be still!

CAPTAIN.

How do you know?

ROSE.

I was once with one of his—relatives, Mrs.
Bleecker.

CAPTAIN.

He is allied to the aristocracy of Manhattan.
Bleecker is a Knickerbocker name! [*Clock strikes.*]

MRS. MONTAGUE.

Eleven !

CAPTAIN.

I did not think it was so late.   Good night !

MRS. MONTAGUE.

I do not need you, Rose.   Good night, uncle.

CAPTAIN.

Good night, my dear.   What a day !

MRS. MONTAGUE.

And what a night !

CAPTAIN.

Oh, yes, the note-book !   [*Laughs.*]   Poor Cuttyback !

> [*Exit L. 1 E.   Mrs. Montague exit R. 2 E.   Rose exit C.   Stage dark and quiet. Door C. opens softly.*

FRANK, *entering C. with casket in his hand.*

It's I.   I am here.   I've found the Paragraph Five.   It was at home in one of my drawers. Here it is.   That Rose is an intelligent girl. Perhaps it is a little late to present one's self in a respectable house.   Especially when one is not invited.   [*Looks at watch.*]   Half-past eleven !

CAPTAIN, *off L.*

The devil take this house !   I can't find my dressing-gown !   Thousand thunders !

FRANK.

The menagerie. On guard! [*Crosses R.*] The dove-cot must be here. My Juliet is the sun —here is the east. [*Lighting gas calmly.*] Josiah Cuttyback, commission-merchant, is a fine fellow. He has excellent taste. Mrs. Montague is a charming woman. [*Reflectively*] Of all wild beasts, woman is the most dangerous. But I have had some experience in the menagerie. Ah! It looks jollier with the lights. Now for business. [*Taps at door R. 2 E., and hides up R.*]

MRS. MONTAGUE, *at door R. 2 E.*

These lights! What can it mean?

FRANK, *coming forward.*

It is I, madam.

MRS. MONTAGUE, *angrily.*

You, sir? Again?

FRANK.

Again, and always!

MRS. MONTAGUE.

Leave the room, sir!

FRANK.

That is impossible, madam, until I have fulfilled my self-imposed mission.

MRS. MONTAGUE, *pointing to Captain's door.*

You will force me to call for aid.

FRANK.

If you but open that cage, madam, you will read in the papers to-morrow : "Yesterday evening a horrible and heart-rending catastrophe occurred in one of our new apartment-houses. A young man, moving in our best society, was devoured by a bloodthirsty wild beast from Brazil in the parlor of Mrs. Montague. It is supposed that the wounds are fatal." Let in the lions, and, like the old gladiators, I shall die saluting thee !

MRS. MONTAGUE.

I like eccentricity and originality. Yours might please me, but not at an hour like this—

FRANK.

I understand and appreciate your scruples. [*Takes and opens screen.*] This divides the room. You remain at home, and I remain at home. We are neighbors, each in his own house. I ask only for five minutes to explain the cause of my return.

MRS. MONTAGUE.

Five minutes ? Well, will you go after that ? [*Frank makes the gesture of an oath.*] Well, then, it is now five minutes to twelve—at midnight you withdraw. [*Sits.*]

FRANK.

In five minutes I shall have fulfilled Paragraph Five.

MRS. MONTAGUE, *smiling.*

You know it, then?

FRANK.

Yes, madam. [*Taking his casket.*] Here it is! [*Sits.*]

MRS. MONTAGUE.

A box?

FRANK.

"Paragraph Five: Burn my love-letters before Mrs. Montague."

MRS. MONTAGUE, *taking note-book from her pocket.*

How did you discover?

FRANK.

A clairvoyant told me—on the staircase. Now to business! [*Takes letter from box.*]

MRS. MONTAGUE.

I scarcely think that I ought to—

FRANK.

It would be neighborly. [*Hands the letter to Mrs. Montague.*] Read! It is very instructive.

MRS. MONTAGUE, *hesitatingly glancing at letter.*

It begins with a burst of passion.

FRANK.

Is there a postscript?

MRS. MONTAGUE.

Yes, about a dress-maker.

FRANK.

There is always a P. S., and generally a dress-maker. [*Leans over.*]

MRS. MONTAGUE.

That's not fair! You are cheating! You said: "Each in his own house!"

FRANK.

I am in my own house—on the balcony. [*Takes another letter*] Number two!

MRS. MONTAGUE, *taking it.*

"I accept your invitation to superr"—one p. and two r's.

FRANK.

She has since married a scene-shifter, rejoicing in the euphonious appellation of J. Stubbs Smith. Number three!

MRS. MONTAGUE, *taking letter.*

Number three is older, I should think.

FRANK.

Yes, she was a widow, grass widow, in weeds,

and wanted me to go without mine. I couldn't
do without smoking, so I did without her. Is
there a P. S. ?

MRS. MONTAGUE, *turning leaf.*
Two !

FRANK.

Of course. The second is merely to keep the
first company. And it was not a good year for
postscripts either. [*Strikes match and lights
packet of letters.*]

MRS. MONTAGUE.

What are you doing ?

FRANK.

I have lighted the *auto-da-fé.* Now Paragraph Five is executed. Mr. Josiah Cuttyback's
day's work is done. See it blaze ! My love-letters have gone to blazes ! Good evening, madam !

CAPTAIN, *off L.*

Thousand thunders ! Where are my slippers ?

MRS. MONTAGUE, *frightened.*

Heavens ! [*Revolver heard off L.*]

FRANK.

It is only your uncle calling for his slippers.

MRS. MONTAGUE.

Fly !
16

FRANK.

Fly ?   Never !

MRS. MONTAGUE.

He will kill you !

FRANK.

You think so ?   All right !   I did not know how to end the day.   Now I am fixed !

MRS. MONTAGUE.

Here he comes !   [*Clasping her hands*]   For heaven's sake, fly, sir !   For my sake, hide yourself !

FRANK, *suddenly inspired.*

Ah ! an idea !   [*Closes the screen around him as Captain enters L. 1 E.*]

CAPTAIN.

How's this ?   You are up ?

MRS. MONTAGUE, *confused.*

Yes, I—I—couldn't sleep, and—and—I had troubled dreams.   I—I—am not at all sleepy !

CAPTAIN.

Nor am I !   Let's have a cup of tea !

MRS. MONTAGUE, *aside.*

Heaven help us !   [*Aloud*] A cup of tea !   At this hour of the night !

CAPTAIN.

Yes !—Rose !

ROSE, *entering C.*

Sir ?

CAPTAIN.

Make us some tea !

ROSE.

Tea ?

CAPTAIN, *shouting.*

Yes, tea !

ROSE, *aside.*

How did he get out ? [*Exit C.*

CAPTAIN, *going to screen and knocking.*

I say, sir, will you have a cup of tea ?

FRANK, *poking head over screen.*

I'd prefer chocolate !

CAPTAIN, *laughing.*

Ah ! Ah ! Ah !

FRANK, *laughing.*

Ah ! Ah ! Ah !

CAPTAIN.

Young man, I like you !

FRANK.

Indeed ! Why didn't you say so before ?
[*Comes out of screen.*] Ahem ! Sir ! As the

custodian of your niece, to whom I have already offered my hand and heart, I ask your permission to pay my ad—

CAPTAIN.

I understand, but my niece's year of mourning won't be over for twenty-two days yet.

FRANK.

We can mourn eleven each!

CAPTAIN, *laughing*.

Ah! Ah! I really like this boy! [*Bell rings.*]

MRS. MONTAGUE.

A visit! at this hour!

ROSE, *entering C.*

It is Mr. Cuttyback.

FRANK.

Probably he has forgotten what time it was!

MRS. MONTAGUE.

I don't want to see him.

CAPTAIN.

His arrival is opportune—

FRANK.

Here, Rose, give him back his overcoat—

MRS. MONTAGUE.

And his note-book!

FRANK.

Permit me. [*Writes in note-book*] "Paragraph Six : Don't bother Mrs. Montague again!" Here, Rose, take it to him! [*To Captain*] One paragraph there refers to you.

CAPTAIN.

What is it?

FRANK.

I'll tell you some day—when we're married. [*Takes Mrs. Montague's hand. Clock strikes twelve.*]

[CURTAIN.]

THE END.

APPLETONS'

New Handy-Volume Series.

Brilliant Novelettes ; Romance, Adventure, Travel,
Humor ; Historic, Literary, and
Society Monographs.

---

10. IMPRESSIONS OF AMERICA. From the "Nineteenth Century." By R. W. DALE. I. Society. II. Politics. III. Popular Education. IV. Religion. 30 cents.

11. THE GOLDSMITH'S WIFE. By Madame CHARLES REY-BAUD. 25 cents.

12. A SUMMER IDYL. By CHRISTIAN REID, author of "Bonny Kate," "Valerie Alymer," etc. 30 cents.

13. THE ARAB WIFE. A Romance of the Polynesian Seas. 25 cents.

14. MRS. GAINSBOROUGH'S DIAMONDS. By JULIAN HAW-THORNE, author of "Bressant," "Garth," etc. 20 cents.

15. LIQUIDATED, and THE SEER. By RUDOLPH LINDAU, author of "Gordon Baldwin," and "The Philosopher's Pendulum." 25 cents.

16. THE GREAT GERMAN COMPOSERS. By GEORGE T. FERRIS. 30 cents.

17. ANTOINETTE. A Story. By ANDRÉ THEURIET. 20 cts.

18. JOHN-A-DREAMS. A Tale. By JULIAN STURGIS. 30 cts.

19. MRS. JACK. A Story. By FRANCES ELEANOR TROLLOPE. 20 cents.

20. ENGLISH LITERATURE. From 596 to 1832. By T. ARNOLD. Reprinted from the "Encyclopædia Britannica." 25 cents.

21. RAYMONDE. A Tale. By ANDRÉ THEURIET, author of "Gérard's Marriage," etc. 30 cents.

22. BEACONSFIELD. A Sketch of the Literary and Political Career of Benjamin Disraeli, now Earl of Beaconsfield. With Two Portraits. By GEORGE M. TOWLE. 25 cents.

23. THE MULTITUDINOUS SEAS. By S. G. W. BENJAMIN. 25 cents.

38. PEG WOFFINGTON. By CHARLES READE. 30 cents.

39. "MY QUEEN." 25 cents.

40. UNCLE CESAR. Ry Madame CHARLES REYBAUD. 25 cts.

41. THE DISTRACTED YOUNG PREACHER, by THOMAS HARDY; and HESTER, by BEATRICE MAY BUTT. In one volume. 25 cents.

42. TABLE-TALK. To which are added Imaginary Conversations of Pope and Swift. By LEIGH HUNT. 30 cents.

43. CHRISTIE JOHNSTONE. By CHARLES READE. 30 cts.

44. THE WORLD'S PARADISES. By S. G. W. BENJAMIN. 30 cents.

45. THE ALPENSTOCK. A Book about the Alps and Alpine Adventure. Edited by WILLIAM H. RIDEING, author of "A Saddle in the Wild West," etc. 30 cents.

46. COMEDIES FOR AMATEUR ACTING. Edited, with a Prefatory Note on Private Theatricals, by J. BRANDER MATTHEWS. 30 cents.

47. VIVIAN THE BEAUTY. By Mrs. ANNIE EDWARDES, author of "Archie Lovell," "Ought We to visit Her?" "Jet: Her Face or her Fortune?" etc. 30 cents.

APPLETONS' NEW HANDY-VOLUME SERIES is in handsome 18mo volumes, in large type, of a size convenient for the pocket, or suitable for the library-shelf, bound in paper covers. A selection may be had of the volumes bound in cloth, price, 60 cents each.

₊ Any volume mailed, post-paid, to any address within the United States or Canada, on receipt of the price.

D. APPLETON & CO., Publishers,

549 & 551 BROADWAY, NEW YORK.

Julian Hawthorne's Novels.

I. GARTH. A Novel. 1 vol., 8vo. Paper cover, 75 cents;
cloth, $1.25.

"'Garth' is Mr. Julian Hawthorne's most elaborate and preten-
tious book. It is on many accounts also his best book, though it contains nothing so good as the character of the hero in 'Bressant.' At
least his genius is unmistakable. And we are disposed to venture the
suggestion that, if 'Garth' had not been a serial, it would have been
more compact and closely written, and so its situations more effective, its characters better sustained."—*New York World.*

II. BRESSANT. A Novel. 1 vol., 8vo. Paper cover, 75
cents; cloth, $1.25.

"We will not say that Mr. Julian Hawthorne has received a double
portion of his father's spirit, but 'Bressant' proves that he has inherited the distinctive tone and fibre of a gift which was altogether
exceptional, and moved the author of 'The Scarlet Letter' beyond the
reach of imitators.

"Bressant, Sophie, and Cornelia, appear to us invested with a sort
of enchantment which we should find it difficult to account for by any
reference to any special passage in their story."—*London Examiner.*

"'Bressant' is a work that demonstrates the fitness of its author
to bear the name of Hawthorne. More in praise need not be said; but,
if the promise of the book shall not utterly fade and vanish, Julian
Hawthorne, in the maturity of his power, will rank side by side with
him who has hitherto been peerless, but whom we must hereafter
call the 'Elder Hawthorne.'"—*New York Times.*

"It will take high rank among the best American novels ever
written."—*Boston Globe.*

"There is a strength in the book which takes it in a marked degree
out of the range of ordinary works of fiction. It is substantially an
original story. There are freshness and vigor in every part."—*Boston
Gazette.*

III. MRS. GAINSBOROUGH'S DIAMONDS. (Form-
ing No. XIV. of Appletons' "New Handy-Volume Series.") 1 vol., 18mo. Paper cover, 20 cents.

D. APPLETON & CO., 549 & 551 BROADWAY, NEW YORK.

CLASSICAL WRITERS.

Edited by JOHN RICHARD GREEN.

16mo. *Flexible cloth.* . . *Price,* 60 *cents.*

UNDER the above title, Messrs. D. APPLETON & Co. are issuing a series of small volumes upon some of the principal Classical and English writers, whose works form subjects of study in our colleges, or which are read by the general public concerned in Classical and English literature for its own sake. As the object of the series is educational, care is taken to impart information in a systematic and thorough way, while an intelligent interest in the writers and their works is sought to be aroused by a clear and attractive style of treatment. Classical authors especially have too long been regarded as mere instruments for teaching pupils the principles of grammar and language, while the personality of the men themselves, and the circumstances under which they wrote, have been kept in the background. Against such an irrational and one-sided method of education the present series is a protest.

It is a principle of the series that, by careful selection of authors, the best scholars in each department shall have the opportunity of speaking directly to students and readers, each on the subject which he has made his own.

The following volumes are in preparation:

GREEK.

HERODOTUS.............Professor BRYCE.

SOPHOCLES..............Professor LEWIS CAMPBELL.

DEMOSTHENES..........S. H. BUTCHER, M. A.

EURIPIDES..............Professor MAHAFFY. [*Ready.*

LATIN.

VIRGIL................Professor NETTLESHIP.

HORACE................T. H. WARD, M. A.

CICERO................Professor A. S. WILKINS.

LIVY..................W. W. CAPES, M. A.

ENGLISH.

MILTON................Rev. STOPFORD BROOKE.
[*Ready.*

BACON.................Rev. Dr. ABBOTT.

SPENSER ....Professor J. W. HALES.

CHAUCER...............F. J. FURNIVALL.

Other volumes to follow.

D. APPLETON & CO., NEW YORK.

WORKS

OF

WILLIAM CULLEN BRYANT.

Illustrated 8vo Edition of Bryant's Poetical Works.
100 Engravings by Birket Foster, Harry Fenn, Alfred Fredericks, and other Artists. 1 vol., 8vo. Cloth, gilt side and edge, $4.00; half calf, marble edge, $6.00; full morocco, antique, $8.00; tree calf, $10.00.

Household Edition. 1 vol., 12mo. Cloth, $2.00; half calf, $4.00; morocco, $5.00; tree calf, $5.00.

Red-Line Edition. With 24 Illustrations, and Portrait of Bryant, on Steel. Printed on tinted paper, with red line. Square 12mo. Cloth, extra, $3.00; half calf, $5.00; morocco, $7.00; tree calf, $8.00.

Blue-and-Gold Edition. 18mo. Cloth, gilt edge, $1.50; half calf, marble edge, $3.00; morocco, gilt edge, $4.00.

Letters from Spain and other Countries. 1 vol., 12mo. Price, $1.25.

The Song of the Sower. Illustrated with 42 Engravings on Wood, from Original Designs by Hennessy, Fenn, Winslow Homer, Hows, Griswold, Nehlig, and Perkins; engraved in the most perfect manner by our best Artists. Elegantly printed and bound. Cloth, extra gilt, $5.00; morocco, antique, $9.00.

The Story of the Fountain. With 42 Illustrations by Harry Fenn, Alfred Fredericks, John A. Hows, Winslow Homer, and others. In one handsome quarto volume. Printed in the most perfect manner, on heavy calendered paper. Uniform with "The Song of the Sower." Square 8vo. Cloth, extra gilt, $5.00; morocco, antique, $9.00.

The Little People of the Snow. Illustrated with exquisite Engravings, printed in Tints, from Designs by Alfred Fredericks. Cloth, $5.00; morocco, $9.00.

D. APPLETON & CO., 549 & 551 BROADWAY, NEW YORK.

APPLETONS' PERIODICALS.

APPLETONS' JOURNAL:
A Magazine of General Literature. Subscription, $3.00 per annum; single copy, 25 cents. The volumes begin January and July of each year.

THE ART JOURNAL:
An International Gallery of Engravings by Distinguished Artists of Europe and America. With Illustrated Papers in the various branches of Art. Each volume contains the monthly numbers for one year. Subscription, $9.00.

THE POPULAR SCIENCE MONTHLY:
Conducted by E. L. and W. J. YOUMANS. Containing instructive and interesting articles and abstracts of articles, original, selected, and illustrated, from the pens of the leading scientific men of different countries. Subscription, to begin at any time, $5.00 per annum; single copy, 50 cents. The volumes begin May and November of each year.

THE NORTH AMERICAN REVIEW:
Published Monthly. Containing articles of general public interest, it is a forum for their full and free discussion. It is cosmopolitan, and, true to its ancient motto, it is the organ of no sect, or party, or school. Subscription, $5.00 per annum; single copy, 50 cents.

THE NEW YORK MEDICAL JOURNAL:
Edited by JAMES B. HUNTER, M. D. Subscription, $4.00 per annum; single copy, 40 cents.

CLUB RATES.
POSTAGE PAID.
APPLETONS' JOURNAL and THE POPULAR SCIENCE MONTHLY, together, $7.00 per annum (full price, $8.00); and NORTH AMERICAN REVIEW, $11.50 per annum (full price, $13.00). THE POPULAR SCIENCE MONTHLY and NEW YORK MEDICAL JOURNAL, together, $8.00 per annum (full price, $9.00); and NORTH AMERICAN REVIEW, $12.50 per annum (full price, $14.00). APPLETONS' JOURNAL and NEW YORK MEDICAL JOURNAL, together, $6.50 per annum (full price, $7.00); and NORTH AMERICAN REVIEW, $10.75 per annum (full price, $12.00). THE POPULAR SCIENCE MONTHLY and NORTH AMERICAN REVIEW, together, $9.00 per annum (full price, $10.00). APPLETONS' JOURNAL and NORTH AMERICAN REVIEW, together, $7.00 per annum (full price, $8.00). NEW YORK MEDICAL JOURNAL and NORTH AMERICAN REVIEW, together, $8.00 per annum (full price, $9.00).

D. APPLETON & CO., Publishers, 549 & 551 Broadway, N. Y.

FAIRY-LAND OF SCIENCE.

By ARABELLA B. BUCKLEY,

Author of "A Short History of Natural Science," etc.

WITH NUMEROUS ILLUSTRATIONS.

12mo. . . . . *Cloth, price, $1.50.*

"A child's reading-book admirably adapted to the purpose intended. The young reader is referred to nature itself rather than to books, and is taught to observe and investigate, and not to rest satisfied with a collection of dull definitions learned by rote and worthless to the possessor. The present work will be found a valuable and interesting addition to the somewhat overcrowded child's library."—*Boston Gazette.*

"Written in a style so simple and lucid as to be within the comprehension of an intelligent child, and yet it will be found entertaining to maturer minds."—*Baltimore Gazette.*

"It deserves to take a permanent place in the literature of youth."—*London Times.*

"The ease of her style, the charm of her illustrations, and the clearness with which she explains what is abstruse, are no doubt the result of much labor; but there is nothing labored in her pages, and the reader must be dull indeed who takes up this volume without finding much to attract attention and to stimulate inquiry."—*Pall Mall Gazette.*

"So interesting that having once opened it we do not know how to leave off reading."—*Saturday Review.*

D. APPLETON & CO., PUBLISHERS, NEW YORK.